Shooting in Buckhead

❚ by Nahid Kabiri ❚

❚ Translated by Sanam Kalantari ❚

Mehri Publication ❚

MEHRI PUBLICATION

Fiction * 8

Shooting in Buckhead

Author: Nahid Kabiri
Translated by: Sanam Kalantari
Edited by: Allen M. Kabiri

British Library Cataloguing Publication Data:
A catalogue record for this book is available from
the British Library | ISBN: 978-1-64945-526-0|
|First Edition. 118 pages | Printed in the United
Kingdom, 2020 | Price: UK £12|

|Book & Cover Design: Mehri Studio|
|Cover Illustration: © Fatemeh Takht Keshian. Ideal-
Ego series. Mixed media on book pages, 2013-16|

www.mehripublication.com
info@mehripublication.com

I

Not many years had passed. It wasn't even seven years. Many things were still new to me. I found some things strange like the rain and windstorms, names I always mixed up. I felt embarrassed to ask again, but you, as always, explained patiently, "Look, the storms and torrential rains you see here that tear everything apart are tornadoes. But hurricanes are common in Florida, where it is near water, because hurricanes get their punch from water." I would hear the wind roaring, branches breaking, windows shattering, my heart pumping, and I would say, "This, I call, the death storm."

The storm that begins with only a few clouds soon turns the sky dark. Then, the wind blows hard, plows the earth, splits giant trees in half and spins them up in the air, twirls heavy cars like toys, lifts people and their wooden homes up into the sky and slams them back to earth.

Well, we had that storm, that year. It was the one. The one that came after you... Who told the storm where you were? The wind blew mercilessly, bent on wrapping around your legs to take you away with it. But when it saw Sara and me next to you, hiding in your arms, it felt sorry for us and left you behind. It didn't overlook our house, though. It ripped the roof off and thrust a large tree with branches and leaves through the pink wall, in Sara's room. It destroyed everything and left a large heap behind: furniture, mirrors, plates, spice jars, knives and forks... We pressed against the wall in the corridor and could hardly breathe from fear.

Moments later, after it whirled around the house and was gone, our gaze met in disbelief. Sara burst out crying, "My doll..."

You dragged us out, I, and Sara in my arms. We hadn't taken more than a few steps when, we heard the walls crashing down. And then, the cry of Sara, and I wailing was lost in the dust, smoke, and the sirens of the fire engines and police cars. We lost you for a moment, too. I shivered in the warm humid air and cried out, "Sohrab... Sohrab!"

Before I lost consciousness, I saw you pushing through the crowd, rushing toward us, clutching Sara's doll in your hands. You pulled me into your arms, the safest place in the world and with your blackened, dusty hands, caressed my hair. You kissed my forehead twice as I looked up at you. You were pale, but had the same warm smile on your lips and the familiar sparkle in your searching eyes. Before I could say anything, you brought your lips close to my ear, "Don't worry, everything will be fine," and then, you went away again.

It was still windy, in the dark I could hear things slamming against things. I looked up at the sky. The moon wasn't out, and a cut cable from a broken streetlamp swung aimlessly between the earth and the sky.

Before the paramedics, oxygen mask in hand, pulling stretchers, reached us, one of the neighbors pointed to Sara and asked how old she was. I hugged Sara and her doll and pressed them against me and said, "Four."

II

The phone rings. I think it is Sara. I kick off my high-heels and run to the phone, "Mom! Have you heard the news? Have you heard what happened?" She sounds excited and out of breath like every time she's about to give me, either good or bad news. "No; what news honey?" She raises her voice, "About the shooting! Last night some crazy person rampaged a movie theater. Do you know how many people he killed?" I collapse into a chair and close my eyes, "Oh my God! Not Again..."

I see myself sitting in that same movie theater with you, watching a love story. Is Sara there too? No, she's not. Sara wasn't born yet. We're sitting snugly, absorbed in the film when, we suddenly hear a burst of gunfire from behind...

Sara pauses; I try to restrain my fear, "Please be careful! Please..." She raises her voice, "What're you talking about Mom?! Do you think the people who were sitting in that movie-theater, watching a comedy, eating popcorn and drinking coke, weren't careful?"

Jahan walks toward me, repeating, "Hannar!" over and over again, but I don't turn around until he taps my shoulder. "Honey, it's getting late. Leave it for later. Hang up please!" he says reproachfully.

I fasten my seatbelt and roll down the window. "Roll it back up please, can't you see I have the AC on?" I roll up the window with such force, that I chip my nail polish.

I am too far from Sara... I am annoyed, that I wasn't able to talk to her properly. I am frustrated. I know she feels the same way, especially today when she's heard the horrible news, that'll be the headline of every newspaper there tomorrow and will leave everyone with a sense of insecurity for a long time again. I wish I could've talked to her more about what happened. I wish I could've told her to leave. America is not the entire world! There are many other wonderful countries too. If you can't change things there, it is best to leave. Like, I did...

The AC circulates the air with the scent of Jahan's cologne. The scent of Hermès. I never knew if Hermès was a philosopher, a prophet, or both. I want to say, "We could've left a little later, so I could've finished talking with Sara." But I don't say anything. I don't ask if, he would've behaved the same way, had Sara been his own daughter. I've wanted to tell him many times, that Sara does not belong on the fringe of my life. That he should be more considerate! But I never have. I show it with my actions though. Some things can't be said out loud. You need a little wisdom and caring to understand.

His mobile phone is constantly ringing. As he honks the horn and speeds up to pass the endless row of cars ahead, he discusses importing bananas and rice with one person and talks about Sunday's bidding and his three-day trip to

Zurich with another. He screeches to a halt at the red light and suddenly remembers there's someone else sitting in the car. "I'm sorry honey! Are you okay?" I don't say anything, nor do I turn to look at him.

We're going to one of those parties again! Boring and stupid ... But the thought of calling Sara later in the night calms me. He parks under a streetlight and turns to look at me, "Wow! You look even more beautiful tonight! But you're a little pale. Why?"

I refresh my lipstick before I step out of the car. The sound of my clicking heels fills the silence in the empty street. One, two, three, four...

It wasn't just three or four people! He killed twenty-two people.... this time in a movie theater, screening a comedy. It wasn't him (Mark!)...No not (Mark Barton!). It was someone like him, what a headline for the morning papers. A terrifying headline. And how could I not be pale Mr. Jahangir Akhavan?! I should've spoken up right there. I should've put down my purse and said, "No! I am not going tonight!" and stayed home.

I should've stayed home and paced the bedrooms and the living room, filled with Baroque furniture, mahogany chests, marble tabletops, and crystals. I should've walked those rooms, adorned with mismatched paintings, until I got dizzy and burst out crying. Yes, I should've cried for those who died in that movie theater. Perhaps, there was a man among them with a wife and a child. He could've been Iranian. Perhaps, his wife was named... I want to go back home so I can pace from one end of the living room to the other. When I feel anxious, staying still makes me feel worse. It's not just me;

someone else has said it before. If I'm not mistaken... no! I'm not mistaken. Milan Kundera said, "When a soul is restless it needs to move." It can't stay still. And if like me, it is forced it into a car and taken to a party, its restlessness worsens.

The living room is teeming with guests. Everyone has arrived. I can't stand any of them though, neither Mr. and Mrs. Sadri, nor their guests. But like a statue, immovable, I take a long-stemmed crystal glass in hand and force a silly smile. I smile, pretending I'm having fun, as if Dr. M's hackneyed jokes are funny, each one funnier than the last!

The lavish appetizer table is refilled over and over again without anyone losing their appetite. The hostess's daughter sits behind the piano, showing off her talents by playing, "Golden Dreams," for the thousandth time. She must be Sara's age. Sara is thinner and she never wears glittery clothes like her and doesn't adorn herself with so much nick-knacks either.

My mind races back to the movie theater that no longer smells of popcorn or coke. Of the victims, how old was the young girl, who on Sunday mornings played the piano with her delicate fingers? or the second year medical student sitting in the third row...? I feel nauseous. I hope the depression that gripped me several years ago doesn't return.

Dinner is announced as soon as I sit down on a sofa. The guests are invited over to a large table laid out in the dinning room. It is covered with such an array of dishes, that not even a tornado could budge it. I gesture to Jahan, asking the time. He looks at his Rolex watch and says, "A little past 10:30; almost twenty minutes to eleven. How come? Are you tired already?" He looks annoyed.

The smell of beef stroganoff, pomegranate stew, shrimp,

fish, kabab, veal, and tongue, grossly mix and hit me, killing my appetite. The music is turned up, as dessert is being laid out, and Jahan is one of the first people to join Mrs. Sadri on the dance floor. As the dance floor fills up, he approaches me panting, but before I can say no, my luck strikes and all the lights go off. It's a power outage. The waiters hurry frantically with candles, lighters, and flashlights. One of them announces the problem is not with the fuse box. Apparently the whole neighborhood is without electricity.

From the full-height windows and the verdant terrace, adorned with a lush garden, bar, ceiling fans, benches, and small tables topped with lit candles, parts of the city sparkle in the distance, a city where secrets and desires are covered in darkness.

As I smile vacantly at the people around me, hardly able to handle the smell of alcohol and cigars, Jahan comes close and kisses me on the cheek.

Some guests have huddled at the bar, and the rest are busy mingling in the living room. Jahan's roaring laughter drowns every other sound. The power comes back on and everyone cheers with joy. We are invited to the dessert table, which includes such delicacies that could please any taste.

After dessert, Mrs. Sadri taps her spoon on the table three times, "Ladies and gentleman, I have an announcement to make!" Dr. F, flanking me, quips, "Make sure you don't burn us!" Everyone laughs inanely. Mrs. Sadri goes on, "There is a talented friend among us tonight who will graciously be charming you with her beautiful voice!" Mr. Sadri blushes; his eyes shine with excitement. He takes over from his wife and continues, "Dear friends, I'm sure you've never heard such a beautiful voice." With mouths full of, sugar powder, whipped cream, chocolate, ice cream, and jelly, the guests look around for a comfortable seat.

My temples are throbbing and my eyes are burning. I am tired and want to say goodbye and go home. I hope the performance doesn't last until two or three in the morning. The hosts' virtuoso friend rises; everyone applauds fervently. She is the young dame who arrived last. She has beautiful auburn hair, long and full. She is wearing a plain skimpy black dress, with two thin straps, delicately tied over her shoulders. "I like to present to you…Nazanin!" Mr. Sadri is at it again, "Of course, we call her Nazy." Wearing thick eyeglasses, Mr. Bakhtiari interjects with his soprano voice, "Sweet Nazy!" Some giggle while Dr. F corrects him, "Beautiful Nazy!" Ms. Parivash rises from her seat, puts her finger against her lips, and says, "Hush!"

Mrs. Sadri asks everyone to applaud, and we do. Nazanin or Nazy picks up her setar and points to the lights in the center of the ceiling. The lights are dimmed. Mr. Shojaie is discreetly jiving with someone, but we can all hear him, "How cozy! It's perfect for a nap!"

Nazanin begins to play with fervor.

III

Most of the guests left after dinner. It was eleven o'clock. The lights were dimed. The rain stopped and a cool breeze rushed in through the windows, ajar. I took off my wedding veil and my shoes. Now we could unwind with our close friends. The official ceremony was lengthy; an American one, followed by an Iranian one. During the Iranian ceremony, we called my parents in Iran and spoke with them and the other guests, who were there. One of our friends filmed the ceremony, and Leila kept walking around me, reminding me not to cry, because it would ruin my makeup.

I looked at you. You were talking to someone on the other side of the living room, and didn't notice my gaze, but since a few hours ago you were my husband. I felt a great sense of joy all over. Your friend, Steve, played many songs that night. When the crowd thinned, he handed you the guitar. I asked Leila, "Does Sohrab know how to play?" She nodded, "He's almost a pro! But he doesn't have much time to play nowadays."

You sat on a barstool, loosened your tie and began to play. You sang a few songs too. You didn't notice me as you were singing. But I was looking at you, discovering more about you with each passing moment. Leila said you also knew a song in Farsi. You didn't want to sing it, because you thought you might've forgotten the lyrics. Leila said, "Hannar may know! She knows a lot of songs. She can sing along if you forget." You paused and then in a low voice said, "In my father's memory." What did you do to me that night? After you sang that song, I felt like I was falling in love with you for the first time, again.

"You have two dark eyes,
You have two..."

You left Iran when you were only four-years-old. You had no memories of the sea, mountains, cities, streets, or the people there. You couldn't even remember your mother, who had left you when you were only six months old. She left you and your father and ran off with a man she loved before your father. You joked, "Well, my mother was beautiful like you and she was fifteen years younger than my father."

Your father divorced her and brought you here to America to live with your aunt.

That night your aunt gave me a pearl necklace and gave you a watch. She turned to me with tears in her eyes, "I fell in love with him the first time I held him in my arms and took him in as a son." You kissed her bony cheek, "I love you Mama-Sha!" She ruptured with laughter and looked at me, "My name is Shah-Sanam, but he called me Mama-Sha as a child!"

We raised our glasses to Leila who had introduced us.

IV

I jolt noticeably when the lights come back on. The melted ice in my glass spills on my dress. A few people notice and grin. Mr. F. quips, "Good morning young lady!" He offers me his white, ironed handkerchief. I stand up. My legs are numb. Perhaps, I did fall asleep. I stretch and see Jahan talking to Nazanin on the other side of the living room. I hear Sara's voice in my head and begin to worry again. I pick up my purse and with heavy steps, walk toward Jahan, "Mr. Jahangir Akhavan!"

V

I was just pregnant when you bought the house. It was on top of a hill, overlooking other houses with colorful roofs, trees, and flowers in backyards. It was like we were submerged in a painting. A few cars passed along the quiet streets, hosting two rows of tall trees. Sparrows and other birds sang for us, filling us with ecstasy. You asked me to look inside the house. It was an old house; the bedrooms, bathrooms, living room, and kitchen, all needed repair. You kept asking if I liked it. What could've I said? I looked at you, trying to muster a word, but you didn't give me a chance, "I'll repair everything, and we'll make a few changes here and there; also don't worry about the mortgage...!"

Hearing about the mortgage petrified me, "I don't mind spending all of our savings on the house, but what about the debt we'll have to bear?" You walked through the empty house, and jested, "Don't worry about owing the bank. It's a debt we'll have to repay for the rest of our lives." Then, you added sardonically, "This is America. We're all in debt for as long as we live!" I looked at you disconcerted, but you laughed louder and came forward and kissed me, "I'm joking! We'll be rich, and we'll be able to pay off the loan early." I wanted to ask how. How were we going to be rich? But I didn't. Later, I learned one way to get rich quick was to dabble in the stock market.

It took a few years before you started that game. You learned the way to that Brokerage House at Piedmont Center. Sara was five-years-old, then. We enjoyed wonderful days and amazing nights under that starry sky... You worked all day long including, Saturdays, and Sundays were never enough to do all that we wanted.

VI

I don't know when Jahan passed by me, went to the kitchen and came back again and presently standing in front of me. He gulps down his glass of water, "You haven't been to bed yet?" I look up the time. It is ten minutes to four. Four A.M. I close my book and head to the bedroom.

Nights like this when much happens, and I hear all sorts of news from here and there, and I have to attend a boring party, where Jahan hands his business card to a young, coquettish girl he's just met, and he's probably planning a party like the one we attend, and he is preparing to go on a short business trip that always lasts longer, and worst of all when several innocent people have lost their lives in a doomed movie theater, and I have to sit still and listen to Sadris' daughter playing the piano off key under blinding chandeliers that feel like interrogation lamps, and the melted ice in my glass spills and stains my brand new dress, and people around me laugh at my gaffe...., I can't sleep! I told the doctor, "I am so tired that as soon as I brush my teeth and go to bed, my eyelids grow heavy, and I fall asleep for half-an-hour or an hour at most, but then, I wake up, and can't fall back to sleep until it's light outside."

The doctor didn't write me a prescription, "You should refrain from taking medication, if possible. Try to spend your nights calmly. Avoid listening to news that upset you. Don't watch exciting films, try to take it easy and cherish your time with your husband." If his beard was any whiter, it would've looked just like my father's; whenever father hugged me his beard tickled my face.

But everything was different that night. When he hugged

me at the airport, his beard was soaked in tear and didn't tickle my face. I never saw him cry before. I looked at Hiva, "Why is he crying? Is it for me or for Sara?" Hiva was tearful too and couldn't speak. I turned to mother, "Please! Tell me if anything has happened!" She shook her head and tried to put on a brave face, "Oh, It's nothing. We've grown used to having you two around. It's difficult being apart," and audibly blew her nose. I jested, "Maybe you know the plane is going to crash and that's why you're crying so hard!" I was angry with everyone and everything, even with my family who were being terribly poignant. I lowered my voice and tried to laugh, "Don't make me regret coming back to visit!" My threat worked and they ceased crying. Father turned to Mother, "She's threatening us as if we're children!"

The airport was heavy with stifling heat. Sara kept pulling on my coat. She wanted to stay with her grandparents, and her aunt Hiva. Hiva pulled my scarf back on my head, "Call us as soon as you get there." I kissed her, "Please go home and take them with you."

I was a couple of years older than Hiva. As children, we used to dress alike. But when we grew older, I broke the habit. We had spats at times and they were invariably my fault. I usually took my anger out on her when adults stressed me. Once I pushed her off the sofa; she was so light and feathery, that she flew on to the floor and scraped her knees. Her chubby, white face turned crimson from crying, and it broke my heart. I held her tight, and said... I can't remember what I said. But I remember my mean mischief. I remember her loud sobs and that still break my heart, especially when I am all alone halfway around the world, musing, and the only sound I hear is the squeaking of the balcony swing, filling the lazy afternoon air. I swing back and forth and whisper over and over again, "Forgive me Hiva!"...Please...

VII

We reach home at the same time. You park next to my car; Sara lets out a happy shriek and lifts her arms toward you. You pick her up and kiss my cheek, "I had a good meeting with the insurance company today. They'll pay us to rebuild the house." I cut you off, "What for? To move back there? I will never go back there..." You point to Sara, hinting to lower my voice, "I know honey. I know. But we have to rebuild the house before we can sell it." I ask, "What about the mortgage?" You laugh, "We still have to pay that! It won't go away by itself. But it's a shame. It was such a great house..."

I say, "I feel safer here in this apartment. No storm can shake us here." You joke, "Don't be so sure. This is America. The United States of America! ..." I pull Sara out of your arms, and mimic you teasingly. Sara is thrilled; she squeals and laughs, which starts us off laughing too.

VIII

Mother keeps raising her voice, asking if I can hear her. I scream, "Yes, yes I can hear you! What is it?" "Do you

remember Ms. Zari? our neighbor across the street?" I think
for a second. I can vaguely remember some things. She had
recently moved there when I was leaving Iran. Mother speaks
with punctuation. She doesn't want me to miss anything.
"Remember I told you that Zari moved back to Iran, and
bought this apartment after her husband died? She's very
lonely, and we see each other quite often. When I showed her
your wedding pictures yesterday, she really liked them and
said you two made a handsome pair. But she kept asking about
the groom. When I said his name was Sohrab Habibi, she
suddenly began to sweat and fainted!" We got disconnected,
"Hello? ... Hello?"

I have to hurry. I'm supposed to meet Sohrab at a
restaurant. It is our first anniversary. But I'm distracted by
mother's phone call. I wonder why she told me all this. What
did the neighbor's passing out have to do with me? Why did
she faint when she heard Sohrab's name? The phone rings
again, "Mother, you were saying?" She's breathing heavily,
"Sorry I hung up. Your father had forgotten his keys, and I
had to open the door for him. Anyway, when she came to,
she said her blood sugar had dropped. She went home but
came back again and explained everything. The poor woman!
Anyway, go tell your husband that her long lost mother has
been found!" She keeps talking, but I'm completely confused,
hazy, and weak by now. She adds, "I always liked this woman.
She is very nice, well-dressed and respectable. But I never
thought that my daughter would someday marry her son on
the other side of the world! And one day we'd be in-laws!"

On the way to meet Sohrab, I kept wondering how and
when to break the news to him. How could I say, "I have
something to tell you honey. Can you believe it? Your mother

lived across the street from us all these years and we never knew!" And, "She has sent you a heartfelt message, asking you to please forgive her..." No! It was too hard to say both parts; the first and the second; the first part about his mother having been found, and the second part about her asking for his forgiveness.

It was early February. I hadn't prepared for my exams yet. I could've found a job at the pharmacy, filling prescriptions, but I preferred to wait another year and continue selling books at Barnes & Nobles. A few days went by, and I had to bear the brunt of mother's daily calls, asking if told Sohrab. I finally felt bad, procrastinating, and said I'd tell him tonight.

I made your favorite spaghetti Bolognese with Portobello mushrooms, and a Greek salad with lots of pepperoncini. You arrived home two hours later. Your working hours were longer than mine. You'd bought me a bouquet of pink and purple Hyacinths. I was ecstatic, and you just stayed there, looking at me, acting crazy. I kept kissing and smelling the flowers, whirling around the room in ecstasy, "Oh my God! This is the smell of spring and love, the smell of the hills, valleys, and gardens of Iran. Thank you Sohrab, I love you!"

You filled the goblets with red wine and put on the reggae CD we had bought in Jamaica. I was already tipsy from the scent of the flowers and slowly moved toward you, to the rhythm of the music. You loosened your tie and joined me. When the music ended, you said, "The spaghetti smells wonderful!" I went to the kitchen and flipped the spaghetti onto a serving dish, "Take a look at the potato crust." I poured the marinara sauce into a bowl and added, "I'll have some good news for you after dinner." When we finished dinner, you turned your chair toward me, "You mentioned good news. Maybe you're gonna say..." You placed your hand on my belly. "No! It has nothing to do with that!"

It was difficult, but I told you. I first beat around the bush a little, but finally came to the point. I spoke, not looking at you, while your gaze was fixed on me and you were in deep science. "Can you believe it?" You shook your head, "No, I really can't believe it. After all these years..." You smirked bitterly, and opened the kitchen window. It was cold outside. The fog covered the top half of your body. I felt bad for you. I went to the bathroom and turned on the faucet. Steam filled the air. You stood there like a mummy. I said, "I've filled the bath tub. It'll make you feel better. Come on..."

The next morning I woke up to the smell of fresh coffee and toast before the alarm went off. You had the breakfast table already set and betrayed a warm smile on your lips. The one I always loved. The one I found on someone else's lips once you took it away from me. On Jahan's lips... Jahangir Akhavan.

You were deep in thought through the following days. You were withdrawn and didn't speak much. I knew your mind was occupied with the shocking news from Tehran... I asked, "Do you want to talk about it?" You shrugged your shoulders and took out a bottle of water from the fridge, "Don't take it too seriously. But sometimes, just sometimes, I think about a ten-day trip. A ten-day trip to, for instance, Tehran!" I sat silently on the sofa next to the window. You raised the bottle of water to your lips, and lowered it again, "But it's still a difficult decision for someone who's been away for so long..." I jumped up excitedly and hugged you. Water was dripping from your hair and you smelled of soap and shampoo. "Let's go for the Persian New Year. It's about a month from now."

Father, mother, Hiva, and Kāk Niāz hadn't met Sohrab yet. They'd be thrilled when they knew we were going to see them. You said, "I have to meet your family someday..."

IX

I hear the door shutting as Jahan leaves the house. I try to fall back to sleep. I wake up to the sound of the bedside phone ringing; it's eleven O'clock! I had forgotten to disconnect it. I can hear Jahan sipping his coffee and sucking on his pipe as he talks. It's something he has recently picked up. He buys his tobacco on his international trips. He mixes three different types of high quality tobacco and sprinkles a few drops of whiskey on them to keep them moist. Each time he lifts the lid off the brown ceramic jar, the scent of fine tobacco and whiskey fill the air. Why did he wake me up? He doesn't have anything important to say. He wants to know why I was sleepless the night before and if I'm feeling better now. I yawn, "Anyone can be sleepless once in a while. It's nothing important." He laughs out loud. I can almost smell his coffee and tobacco through the phone and it makes me cough.

I have to pack his suitcase. I also have to do some grocery shopping and cooking. I've kept my book on the kitchen counter, so I won't forget to start translating it. I procrastinate, all the time.

This sort of life perturbs me. I'm always worried about something. I wonder if it's because of Jahan. If he is the one who gives me anxiety. Sometimes I can't handle all the plans he makes. I used to complain, "You make me confused with your plans, trips, friends, parties, meetings, and constant hopping from one place to another." But I've stopped saying anything anymore, because it is useless. I wonder what role I play in his life. Why has he brought me here all the way from the other side of the world? to do what? to wait? To wait until he looks at me with that mesmerizing smile, driving me crazy? To look at me with his beautiful eyes, giving me butterflies? To assure that nothing is wrong? To have him call my name with his husky voice, to assure me that everything is like it was, and he is none other than you, and I haven't mistaken him as anybody else? He is you....

X

We spend the last Sunday before our trip strolling in the park near our house. The smell of barbeque from nearby houses fills the air. You look at me, "I'm getting hungry!" and I meet your eyes, "This park smells of life, it smells of love..." You take a deep breath, "Yes. It feels like there are people around here who are enjoying their moments. That's what life is all about, all those little precious moments that compound to form a life."

I say, "Sundays here, remind me of Fridays in Iran. When we lived in Kurdistan, we used to take big pots of food and go to grandfather's orchard every Friday. Aunts, uncles, and cousins would come in droves. Grandfather's orchard was always filled with fruit: cherries, peaches, apples, plums...

the plums were juicy and sour. We ate them with salt, which dulled our teeth all day long. We sang, danced and played stunts the whole day long." I notice you look at me with envy. It breaks my heart, because you don't have any memories of your family. I shouldn't tell you all these things. You stand squarely in front of me and pull me toward yourself. You bring your lips to my cheek and whisper in my ear, "When we come back from Iran, we'll take out a loan and we'll buy a house. A big, bright house with a garden, porch, grille, and a beautiful baby that'll look just like you..." Your breath smells like mint gum. I close my eyes and imagine a three-bedroom house on top of a hill. The same one the wind dug out of the ground and crushed, but left the geraniums and petunias we'd just planted, untouched. And the day after the storm, the flowers shone even brighter than ever, under the blue, blue sky...

XI

You carry the suitcases and put them in the trunk, "Why are they so heavy? What've you put in them?" I shrug my shoulders, "It's all the books and souvenirs."

You don't seem well this morning and it seems you're looking for an excuse to cancel the trip. On the way to the airport we argue over petty stuff. I say, it is easier to call a cab, but you don't agree, "What's wrong with taking the car? We'll only be gone for a week and can leave the car in the airport parking."

We're both anxious about the trip. But you are more

anxious than I am. You are going to a country where nothing will be familiar to you. You'll meet a woman who, is and isn't, your mother. And you'll see a house that you've no memories of. I look at your face. It is tense and sweaty. You're clutching the wheel with a frown on your face, staring out at the far distance, along Interstate 285. Your tension rubs off on me too. To help me relax, I try to think of Iran and all the warmth, affection, and hospitality we'll be received with, there.

A few days ago you asked if I had made hotel reservations. I couldn't believe it! I warned you, "I hope you don't mention this again, because it will offend my family, and will break their hearts. Hiva said they had prepared the master bedroom for us. They had bought a new mattress, a velvet bedspread, and new sheets for us. Mother is a tasteful woman. I was sure she had, elaborately, prepared for our arrival.

XII

I've been calling since 10 A.M. her time, but Sara is not answering. I feel uneasy again. I've left her four messages, "Sara pick up. It's me."

I know she doesn't have class for another two hours. I don't know any of her neighbors to ask to check on her. It feels like, a flock of birds have been trapped in my chest and won't stop flapping their wings. My mouth is parched and I can hear my heart pounding. I can't sit still. I keep wiping the kitchen table and finally drop my coffee cup on the floor, shattering into a thousand pieces of all sizes. I try to carefully pick up the larger pieces with my fingers, so I can sweep the rest with a broom. I cut my finger on a sharp piece. Ouch… I turn the faucet on. The water running on my cut burns my finger, but stops the bleeding. I wrap my finger with some tissue and run toward the phone ringing off the hook. It must be her, Sara…

Oh! Why did I pick up! I shouldn't have. Now I have to go through this decorous chitchat. Yes! Thank you! No, thank you! No, he's not home. I'll let him know. Sure!

I go back to packing the suitcase, but I can't concentrate. I can't remember what I have to pack. Once again I walk to the phone. Whenever my grandmother lost something or felt anxious about someone being late, she pledged fourteen litanies, invoking divine providence. With pleading eyes, staring up at the sky, she recited seven prayers, but kept the remaining seven for after her prayer was answered. I learned that prayer early on, a prayer that worked for every crisis! A miracle cure for all urgent cases.

I hang up the phone and begin pacing the room, feverishly reciting grandmother's seven prayers. Then I lift the receiver and dial the number again, beep…beep…beep… the same answering message, followed by a long beep, and an ominous silence. I wonder what I'll do if I don't hear from her by tomorrow. What would I really do? Leila didn't live in Georgia anymore and had taken Mama-Sha with her. She had told me angrily, "We hope to never pass under Atlanta's sky again."

I take a few deep yogic breaths. It doesn't help. I lie down on the floor, place my hands on my abdomen, and focus on my breathing. I follow every inhale down into my diaphragm and every exhale back up again. But it's useless. My breathing is uneven, and I feel like suffocating.

I occupy myself with the suitcase again packing pants,

shirts, underwear, and socks, enough for four days. I leave other items like toothpaste, toothbrush, and cologne for later. He'll pick out his own ties. I go to the kitchen and make some salad dressing. The potatoes are already cooked; I'll braise the fish in olive oil after Jahan arrives and while he's taking a shower and making a few calls.

The doorbell and the phone ring all at once. I feel like this time the ring sounds different. I open the door for Jahan with one hand and pick up the phone with the other. "Sara! Where've you been? I've been worried sick!" Her greeting is cut short by a long yawn, "Why've you called so many times? I was asleep! I was working on Mat's project till three in the morning. And I couldn't fall asleep until eight in the morning, because I drank too much coffee. So what's going on?" I don't know what to say. I feel embarrassed. Feelings of elation and calm race to fill me up from head to toe. Sara raises her voice. Maybe I've upset her again with my phone calls. "Hello? ... Did you say something?" Maybe I had muttered, "Thank God!" I said, "No, I didn't say anything. I just wanted to know how you were."

She sounds tired and touchy, "Okay! Later..." I remain silent and she doesn't hang up, "So what's new? Say something! How are you? How is Jahan?" I am happy that she cares about how I am. And I am happier that she is okay, "I'm just fine darling. I love you so much. That's all!" She is silent. I feel like she is disappointed in me again for calling her so many times, like a stalker. "Please don't call so many times. It makes me worried. I think maybe there's been an earthquake, or someone has died, or something..." I blurt a laugh, and she finishes, "Okay, I've got to go. Love you!" Before she hangs up, I rush to say, "I love you too sweetie!"

The vinaigrette salad dressing is way too salty, but Jahan

talks about his business plans and new contracts with the Swiss so excitedly, that he doesn't even notice. I manage to keep a silly smile and nod my head, but my mind is far away.

I raise a glass of water and swallow my pills. Jahan shakes his head, "Are you still taking pills?" I reply, "Just a few. It's for my anxiety." He leaves the table. I continue in a louder voice, "I had stopped taking them, but started again the night I heard about the student who shot his teacher!" Jahan sits down again and stares deep into my eyes, "What's that got to do with us Hannar? Why do you care about things that happen halfway around the world? You left that place so you won't hear about those things anymore. So you won't have to take pills anymore. Why does Sara keep telling you this stuff? Is she stupid or what?!" I almost yell, "Jahan!..."

He looks at his watch. We both get up. I wasn't listening to anything he was saying and I feel bad. I am always distracted when he talks; thinking about other people and other places and I feel guilty about it. I am ashamed of the distance between us. He drags the suitcase to the front door and speaks kindly, "I've made a guest list. It's on the fridge. Please start calling them on Wednesday to invite them for the 20th. Make sure you invite Nazanin too." The driver presses the buzzer. Jahan starts toward me. I close my eyes to better savor the familiar scent of his cologne...

XIII

I loved the scent of your cologne. I remember where and when you bought it. We always had dinner together and talked, and talked. We had so much to talk about. You translated some of the English words I couldn't understand, and I laughed at some of the Farsi words you used out of context, correcting your mistakes. We were, alternatingly, teacher and pupil.

You always filled my glass first. Whenever you sat across from me, I forgot everyone and everything; it was like nothing else existed. You sometimes played the guitar and sang the songs I liked, songs like, "Nights in White Satin", and, "Never Gonna Let You Go". And we continued talking afterwards. We talked about our upcoming trip to Iran. The following day was a Saturday, and I wanted to buy the souvenirs we were going to take with us. I reminded you, "We have to buy something for your mother too." You looked vacantly in the distance and smiled. The same smile that I love, the one that has brought me to the house of a man, who has a smile just like yours. You said, "I really don't know what to get her. Not clothes! I don't even know if she is fat or thin!" I ask my mother. "Zari is neither fat nor thin. Buy her something medium." We go to a perfume shop. You pick a perfume for me, one for your mother, and a cologne for yourself. The same cologne Jahan wears...

XIV

Jahan walks out the door and I head to the window. The driver takes the suitcase and Jahan sits in the backseat. With his overcoat and the knit scarf covering his neck, and the way he walks, his silhouette is just like yours. It's like you're the same person, with broad shoulders and those long, strong legs. The driver makes a U-turn and the car disappears out of sight. Silence fills the house, and the only sound I can hear is the ticking of the clock.

XV

You never travelled anywhere without me and didn't spend hours in different cafés meeting other people, like Jahan does. I was part of all your plans, and involved in all your meetings. You had a stable job with a set income. It was enough to allow me to stop working and instead focus on my studies in my final two years at the university. But I continued working part-time and enjoyed it too. I enjoyed working, I enjoyed studying, I enjoyed life, and I enjoyed you... even the hours you sent me to the bedroom to study and you sat in front of the TV, reading a book. When tired, I called you into the room to ask a question, and you always explained everything like a serious professor. I took notes quickly, and before you'd leave, I'd grab your hand, "I'm tired professor. Let's leave the rest for later..."

XVI

After Jahan left, I felt depressed. I was left again in this big house, filled with oversized rugs, glittery furniture, and démodé paintings... I didn't feel any less alone when he was around either. But at least I was busy and felt more secure.

I told the doctor, "How can I explain? His comings and goings keep me busy. The phone rings constantly when he's around. He eats with gusto and loves frequenting fancy restaurants. He loves fresh flowers, classical music, expensive clothes, glitz and glamour." The doctor looked at me kindly, "And? Continue!" I took a sip of water, "I know these are all part of life, but there is a sense of emptiness, as if this life is built on emptiness, not happiness." When I was riding back in the taxi, I felt embarrassed by my paranoia and silliness.

I woke up to the sound of the street sweeper's broom, scraping the ground, which always announced his arrival at 6 a.m. It was too early to be up. I'd had a late night. Jahan's side of the bed was covered in a heap of papers, books, a few dictionaries, and my laptop.

I felt the books and papers with my hands, as I lie under the warm covers with my eyes shut. In my mind, I could even read the last few lines I had translated the night before. I felt content that I had finally begun work on an interesting book. Jahan had stuck the guest list on the fridge. I knew everyone more or less, except for his guest of honor, Nazanin, who was Mrs. Sadri's best friend.

I stared at each name, and imagined their faces, the women with their coiffed hairdos, and heavily powdered faces, and the men who all looked alike with their silky clean-shaven faces, neatly groomed hair, and pricy Italian designer ties.

The only odd person among the group was Nazanin. Maybe she was drawn unwantedly into the group, just like

I was. I remembered that she had arrived at the party alone. Since we hadn't even exchanged a single word, I had no desire to call and invite her over to dinner, to have her play the Setar and sing and laugh at our friends' silly jokes and steal their hearts with her coquetry, especially Mr. Jahangir

Akhavan's heart!

I thought it over for a couple of minutes and left the kitchen. But a few hours later when I couldn't concentrate on my work anymore, I returned to the kitchen and picked up the phone. I told myself that thinking about some things is harder than actually doing them. I had to finish this task as soon as I could, so I'd return to chapter two of my book. And later in the afternoon, after working for a few more hours, I would push the furniture out of the way, turn up the music, change into walking shoes, and walk around the living room without having to worry about the Islamic covering I'd need to wear out on the street. I'd finish the day with a steamy shower, a light dinner, and a film I'd wanted to see for some time.

As soon as I began to introduce myself, Nazanin laughed warmly. She had a kind, sweet voice, "... yes! You're Hannar. Your husband called from Zurich a couple of hours ago. It'll be my pleasure to join you!"

Night slowly slipped into the room. It was already dark before I rose to turn on the lights.

Jahan had called several times already, but I didn't pick up. I didn't feel like hearing his voice, even though he sounded just like you, which always puzzled me as to how he'd stolen your voice from you. What did he want to say anyway? I pick up the phone, "No, not at all. I'm not bored. I've been quite busy. I've already finished half of the book."

He talks of here and there, of the wonderful entrecote

steak he has enjoyed with his new Swiss friends, of the fresh cool air that energizes him and the new red suede coat he has bought for me.

Before hanging up I say, "You've already called and invited her. I'm talking about Nazanin!" He pauses for a few seconds. "Yes, I wanted to make sure she comes, we have to have live music." I don't care about anything else he says. I only want to say, "I miss your voice honey, keep talking." But I don't. I say goodbye instead and hang up.

XVII

We return from Iran. The bookstore manager has changed and I don't like working with the new manager. You want me to spend all my time, focused on my last two years at the university. That spring and summer, I study hard and you work hard, which brings us closer and closer to buying the house we dreamed.

It's like it was only yesterday when you walked in like a hero, calling my name, "Hannar! Hannar! It's done! We're buying the house! The one you fell in love with. The bank has approved our loan. Take a look!" I look at the letter of approval, signed and sealed. I am numb and can't utter a single word. My mind is on my test results. You stand before me motionless, looking at me without blinking an eye. "Aren't you happy?" Like a helpless child, I hide myself in your arms and burst into tears. You are confused and worried, "Hannar? What's wrong?" I manage a laugh and take something out of my purse. "I have a surprise too!"

What a strange night it was. We didn't know what to do with all the excitement we felt. In one single night, we had become both parents and home owners.

XVIII

From the hot roaring convection oven, I pick out the bulky Idaho potatoes that have been cooked to perfection with their skin on, stuff them with beef stroganoff, chicken a la king, steamed broccoli, or cauliflower and then put them in a smaller broiler oven, for another thirty seconds. On the veggies, the customers can choose to add, smoked Wisconsin cheese sauce, shredded cheddar, bacon bits, ranch dressing or chives.

You make me nervous when you show up unexpectedly. You squeeze in line with the other customers, so I don't notice you, until you suddenly appear in front of me and say, "One potato with broccoli and cheese sauce and no butter please, ma'am!"

I lift my head and we both burst out in laughter and I hurry to prepare your food. Sometimes, I am so distracted by your showing, that I burn my fingers, "Here you go!" You take the plate and surreptitiously put a small box wrapped in pink paper with a silver bow in my hand. I lift my hand to my mouth to keep me from making a sound. The store manager says, "Next please!" and you hurry away. I turn around and slip the present inside my bra, so I can feel it against my skin.

It is almost 3:30 in the afternoon, time for my lunch break. Most of the tables are empty now. I pick a table behind a column and sit down. I'm famished, but I open your gift first. On a small piece of paper you've scribbled, "I love you". It is a designer necklace of two delicate, interweaved hearts in gold. I pop open the clasp and hang it around my neck with care.

I tie the bow around the empty box and begin eating my lunch, a fruit medley salad of chopped apples, red grapes, and juicy pineapples. I'm so hot on busy days that I prefer a cold fruit salad to a warm lunch. I place my hand on my belly and feel the heartbeat of the beautiful creature that'll be breathing and smiling in six months, sharing our home with us.

I'm deep in my dream when ... the sudden sound of bullets fired, hangs my world on its orbit, in suspension, time comes to a halt. Someone yells, "Get down...get down on the floor!" I hear more shots fired and the sound of a police whistle...and mayhem....I slip onto the floor with the chair and table turning over...

Someone helps me up. At first I think I'm dead, then, I feel like I'm asleep, having a nightmare. It seems like a deep sleep and I hesitate to wake up from it. I'm in an ambulance and someone is taking my blood pressure. He says, "Don't worry, you'll be fine." A telephone rings, "It's over. No one has died. The police got him, took away his gun and arrested him."

The doctor looks over the test results and after examining me carefully he assures you that both the mother and child are well. But you are distressed and still in shock. You ask my boss for a week off.

XIX

Mother, burns incense, and wafts the smoke around my head to keep away evil eyes, "Her eyes were big and black and shone like stars when she was born." Father cuts her off, "That's why we wanted to name her Ghazāl (gazelle) at first, because of her eyes." She continues, "Then, we decided to call her Reyhan, or as said in our dialect, Rian. It's a beautiful name, but we ended up calling her Hannar..." Your silky gaze locks with mine; I am embarrassed and blush. I try to change the topic, "Tell Sohrab what the Kurds wash their hair with." Mother snaps, "They wash their hair with sour milk. But not the fizzy kind they sell in stores in Tehran!" We all laugh. Father puts aside his newspaper and says, "Churned sour milk! All natural! If you stay longer we can go visit the region - Kāk-Zorav." He smiles, and mother explains that Kurds pronounce Sohrab, as Zorav. She turns toward Kāk-Niāz, "Isn't that right?" Kāk-Niāz keeps spinning the smoking incense around our heads and returns, "That's absolutely right."

I say, "I can still taste the fresh butter they make from churned sour milk. The most delicious butter in the whole world..."

You take my hand and kiss it gently, "You are just like a child my Ghazāl!" Hiva cuts in, "Your Farsi has improved. Hannar must be a good teacher. The last time we spoke on the phone you had difficulty with your Farsi."

Mother leaves the room and my father picks up his newspaper again. I gesture to Sorhab to get up, "We're going to take a nap. Hiva, will you please remember to wake us up at five? We have plans for the night." We hadn't slept a wink the night before. You were anxious about seeing your mother, and your anxiety had seeped through to me too.

We were flying over the Atlantic Ocean when you admitted you regretted coming on this trip. You felt you'd made a rash decision and were afraid of seeing your mother, who was still a stranger to you. You didn't touch your dinner tray. I said, "It's not too late honey. Would you like me to tell them we'll be getting off here?" You looked at my serious face and started to laugh. I leaned against your arm, and you finally finished your dinner.

You keep turning and twisting under the crisp sheets. You are restless and I can't help you. You keep thinking perhaps it would've been better if you had left things the way they were, that seeing your mother after all these years wouldn't change anything, especially now that your father was dead. They told you he slipped and fell off the mountain on an early November morning, but you knew that he had jumped off. He was in love with your mother and couldn't bear the pain of losing her.

I run my fingers through your hair and gently massage your scalp, and you close your eyes and fall asleep for a little while. But I can't close my eyes, even though I am exhausted. I keep thinking about your father and how he killed himself over his unfaithful wife. Just like Sappho, the poetess did when she was rejected by Phaon. The only difference was that Sappho was a woman in ancient Greece, and Saeed Habibi was a man in Tehran. I've seen a few pictures of him and remember that his eyes were green, just like yours. Apparently he had a nice voice and sang too, and you had heard him sing, "Those Black Eyes" many times. He must've cried also when you weren't around.

Your aunt said that one year after he left you with her in

America he sold his house in Nishapur and sent you all the money. He was left with only a bookstore. Your father was a renowned publisher. She heard that after selling his house, he had to sleep in a small room in the back of his bookstore. One day he asked his friends to put everything up for sale and then, left for Tehran without telling anyone. He decided to put an end to his misery on the heights of Mount Damavand.

Your aunt said after your mother left him and after he left you in America, that athletic, energetic man was reduced to lifeless stone. He couldn't move and spent all day in bed, leaving others to take care of things. She heard he couldn't even bring himself to reach the refrigerator. In a way he had turned into the character, Oblomov in Ivan Goncharov's novel. Of course she didn't say this. It is just my assumption!

XX

Although, Jahan's presence meant more chaos and non-stop comings and goings, it upset me when he called to say his trip was extended by a few days. I must've loved him unknowingly. Or perhaps, I was just bored and preferred having him around. In any case, Jahan wasn't my whole life and he shouldn't have been. I never wanted to betray you. You and Sara had filled my life, and how sad that the three of us were separated from each other. I have to admit that Jahan was part of my life too, but he only had a defined share in my life. Without him, I would've lost you forever and would've been dead, or I'd be spending my life in an asylum in America, more dead than alive.

I call Sara. "We're coming over this summer. Jahan says he misses you too." These were not his words, they were mine. She is happy, "Your room is just like it was!" The way she talks, sometimes reminds me of you, it brings smile to my lips. I say, "We're not going to disturb you each time we come to visit." She says reproachfully, "Did you learn these silly formalities from the Iranians?" I laugh, "I am an Iranian after all!"

We switch to English without thinking about it, even though she understands Farsi quite well. I told Jahan we only spoke Farsi with her when she was a child; he couldn't believe it. Her connection to her mother tongue became less and less after she started school.

Jahan says, "Your English is not English, it is American. You drop the beginnings and endings of sentences, which is confusing." I want to say he should live in America for a while to know better, but I don't. I don't tell him that I don't understand him or the way he speaks Farsi.

I sometimes think he is such an unusual person, so terribly complicated. For instance when he first hired Shirin as a secretary, he used to praise her qualities all the time. He'd say, "She doesn't care for everyone, but she really likes you. She's into books and translating, like you are." He promised me an office at the firm so I could do my work from there. I was happy by the offer, because I could never get any serious work done at home.

The day I went to the office with my books and dictionaries, Jahan wasn't there. Shirin said something had come up and he had to leave. She brought me coffee and sat with me. "Didn't he tell you? We hired a new accountant a few days ago. He began working in that room today." Then, she offered me her own office and tried to change the subject.

Jahan was unfazed, "Believe me, I wasn't told. Shirin hired the accountant. I've given her too much authority. She's taking advantage of it." But it was nonsense. Shirin was a smart girl. She knew her job and managed the firm well. I felt like she knew Jahan better than I did. She had a cute mouth and luscious lips and spoke well. Her mother was from Tajikistan. I said, "So that's where you get your beauty." She laughed. She knew English, French, Spanish, and some German and I was sure she played an important role in managing his contracts and business relations with his international clients.

We grew closer every time we met. She often worked on weekends too, writing letters that she brought home for Jahan to sign. I prepared tea or coffee and had her stay longer, "With all the work you do when, can you find time to read?" She had read "Memories of My Melancholy Whores" by Marquez in Spanish and Moliere's poetry in German and I was ashamed that I hadn't even finished university!

Jahan never joined our conversations when Shirin came over. He either stayed in the library or went downstairs to the swimming pool and hot tub and enjoyed a massage by Susan who came on the weekends. And when Jahan came back upstairs, like I said, she was a smart woman, she picked up her purse and left. Jahan didn't want to see her too often. He complained, "She philosophizes about everything! I don't want to see her on the weekends too! Weekdays are enough."

Hiva called once or twice a week from Canada. Mother had gone to visit her and Sara a couple of months ago. She had to renew her Green Card every six months. I promised to take care of father while she was gone. Father couldn't handle travelling anymore, but he never kept mother from going either. He said she should go visit the children. He said Kāk-Niāz can take care of him. I told Hiva about Shirin, and she was happy that I had finally found a friend. She asked me about Shirin today. "She's fine. She was just here and we had a nice, long chat. She brought me two books to see if I like to translate."

I feel like Hiva, mother, and Sara aren't much worried about me. They think everything is dandy, and with Jahan around, I am all set. They don't realize what a complicated man he is. Sometimes I feel like I barely know him. At first, he encouraged me to befriend Shirin, but recently it seems that he doesn't approve of our friendship. But I don't care, because nothing is that important to me anymore. I hoped to someday, meet someone, whom I could talk to about you, about the secret... about the things that have leaked from you to Jahan. About the secret that no one knew and wouldn't understand anyway.

XXI

Sundays ... those golden Sundays ... when the sun spreads into our bedroom and kitchen, and sparrows hop from branch to branch, shaking ripe black mulberries off the trees. And I smell the sweet scent of the earth, as Sara wakes up and claws at my breasts hungrily. You put on the floral apron and begin cooking in the kitchen. You were an expert, cooking Italian food, and at first I wondered if you had ever worked in a restaurant, or taken cooking classes. As you chop a bunch of basil you laugh and reply, "Many people have thought so!"

I don't like the sound of your nostalgic laugh or the way you say, "Many people." "So you mean many people..." You laugh louder, "What? What're you trying to say?"

You don't seem to mind being reminded of your American girlfriends, like Kristine whom you said looked like, Jacqueline Kennedy, or the other one, your classmate, whose name I've forgotten... aha! Anna ... the one from Rome, no, from Florence.

Sara has fallen asleep at my breast. I gently pull down my shirt and get up, annoyed. You untie the apron and say, "What's wrong? Did you get upset?" I go into the bedroom, "I'm tired. I'm gonna lie down a little." You come closer. Your breath smells of fresh basil.

I have to be alone for a while to calm down. I'm ashamed of myself for my silly jealousies when there isn't the slightest trace of deceit in your entire being.

XXII

I woke up in the middle of the night to the sound of running water. I sat up in bed, terrified, and held the covers against my mouth to keep me from screaming ... No I wasn't mistaken. The sound came from the master bathroom. Jahan wasn't supposed to come back for another week and he never showed up without notice. I went toward the light shining from the living room, and relaxed after a few steps. Jahan's suitcase was in the middle of the living room and his clothes were scattered everywhere. My knees were still shaking and I went into the kitchen to get an apple and a glass of water. Jahan suddenly hugged me from behind, wearing only a bathrobe, "Good morning darling!" I let out a shriek, followed by laughter. His hair was still wet, and water was dripping down my neck. "You're such a heavy sleeper. You wouldn't have woken up if I'd been a burglar!" For a second I thought what if it was Mark Barton in the shower...

He took the glass of water and the apple from my hands. I meant to say, "You weren't supposed to come back tonight" or "Why didn't you tell me you were coming" or "You scared me," but instead, I brought my hand to my mouth and yawned. He said, "I wanted to surprise you."

Back in bed, I just wanted him to keep talking. I wanted to close my eyes and hear his voice. I put my head on his chest and said, "I really missed you. Keep talking so I can fall back to sleep."

Rested and relaxed, we had breakfast around noon. The scent of fresh ground coffee filled the kitchen. The phone rang, and Jahan picked it up. I began to review my shopping list for the party, and added cocktail olives to the list. Jahan said, "Hang on. Speak to his daughter." It was dreadful news! He wasn't feeling well and had a fever again. Jahan took back the receiver and hung it up. "You didn't tell me your father was in the hospital." I hurried to the bedroom to get dressed. "Have you told your mother and Hiva?" I replied, "Not yet. I don't want to worry them."

He sat on the edge of the bed. "Do you need me to..." I cut him off, "Not yet." As I sped through the congested streets to reach Sadr Highway, I talked to Kāk-Niāz twice on the phone.

It seemed as if the distance to the hospital kept stretching endlessly. I crossed Abbas-Abad intersection, passed Takht-e-Tavoos St., Kooh-e-Noor St., and finally reached the hospital on Jam St. As usual, a crowd of people carrying fresh bouquets and boxes of pastry were swarming around the elevator, which seemed to be stuck on the fifth floor. I hurried up the stairs instead.

When I went to visit him at home yesterday afternoon, the TV was on and Kāk-Niāz had put a cup of tea, some biscuits, and some apple puree on the table in front of him. I said, "Hi!" But he didn't turn to greet me like he always did, "Well hello my sweet princess! When did you get here? Welcome, welcome!" I walked toward him. He had fallen asleep in front of the TV, flickering on and off. I turned it off. Kāk-Niāz came in holding a tea tray. "He hasn't been feeling well all morning. And you saw how he didn't have any appetite yesterday." I began to rub his shoulders to slowly wake him up. I caressed his hair. His forehead was warm, but I wasn't sure if he had a fever.

I said, "Hi! It's me!" He woke up. I brought the glass of water close to his lips, but he couldn't swallow and kept coughing. It seemed like his throat was blocked. I said, "Kāk-Niāz let's go. Hurry up!" Luckily it was a Wednesday, and the doctor saw patients at the hospital clinic until 8 p.m.

We had him ready and put him in the car. Kāk-Niāz sat in the back next to him and mumbled, "It's getting harder and harder to move him." I looked at father in the rearview mirror and then looked at Kāk-Niāz. "The doctor told us this would happen. Don't you remember? He said as he loses his memory his muscles grow tight and heavy." Kāk-Niāz wiped a tear with his sleeve and I started the car.

The waiting room was bustling with patients, fidgeting in

their seats, impatiently waiting for their names to be called. I didn't take my eyes off of father, who was resting his head on Kāk-Niāz's shoulder. He had on his pressed blue shirt and dark blue pants, but he missed a tie around his neck. Father usually wore a tie in the afternoons, in case anyone came to visit him, but no one came anymore. Before we left the house he held out his left arm, waiting for me to put on his watch. Then he put his hand in his pocket, looking for something. "Are you looking for your wallet? I have it here," I pointed to my purse. Kāk-Niāz said, "No, he wants his handkerchief." He took a neatly folded handkerchief out of the dressing table drawer and put it in father's pocket.

The waiting room wasn't hot, but father kept trying to wipe off his sweaty forehead with his handkerchief. His eyes were droopy and he was coughing uneasily. I tried to help him, but he pushed my hand away. The receptionist finally called our name, "Dr. Marzban!" The doctor said it would be best if he stayed in the hospital for a few days. But he didn't tell us how bad things were.

When I reached the last floor I was out of breath. The door to room 401 was half open and Kāk-Niāz was awkwardly napping in a chair. "When did his fever rise?" Kāk-Niāz's face was drawn and his eyes were bloodshot, "Early this morning." Father was breathing rapidly. His eyelids looked heavy. An IV slowly delivered fluids through his vein, drop-by-drop. "Why didn't you call sooner?" I could barely hear him, "I didn't want to wake you up. I informed the nurse instead."

He didn't know that Jahan hadn't let me sleep all night. He didn't know that when he thought I'd taken a pill and gone to bed, Jahan had arrived unexpectedly and I had forgotten all about my sick father. The guilt I felt nauseated me. I felt sorry for my father, who was burning with fever, and didn't know what I could do for him.

The sky wasn't visible from the window. A mélange of short and tall, ugly buildings made of dull brick and concrete, adorned with a myriad of stained satellite dishes, had swallowed up the sky. I looked left and right hopelessly, trying to find a tiny bit of sky, so I could pray to God, "My father! Dear God, my father!" As a child I was told that God lived in the sky, behind the clouds. And we always blew our prayers up to the sky, toward a mysterious blue, gray, or black unknown.

Jahan said he'd let Hiva know, but I wasn't sure what to do about Sara. How could I tell her grandfather was dying? "When I come to Iran I'll stay with grandfather." Her presence had uplifted my father for a long time. Until recently, each time I saw father, he recounted everything Sara had told him, word by word. Every day, he asked, "When is she coming back?" I'd say, "Sara?" and he'd nod his head.

It was 9 p.m. when Jahan showed up. I wondered where he'd been all this time. I had sent Kāk-Niāz home to rest up, so he'd be able to handle another sleepless night. I looked at Jahan's clean-shaven face. He wore a brand new white shirt that he had probably bought on his recent trip. I said, "I wish you hadn't put on cologne. It's not good for his lungs." He didn't hear me, or pretended not to. "What's new? Did the doctor come to see him?" I had a lump in my throat and my voice sounded unfamiliar, "Yes, a few hours ago. He said there is fluid in his lungs. He told us to pray for him." Jahan let out a wry laugh, "What a doctor! If he tells you to pray it means it's the end!"

Kāk-Niāz walked in quietly, "Hello. He's not up yet..." It

was neither a question nor a comment. He was simply talking to himself and didn't expect anyone to answer. His crimson eyes told he had been crying, or maybe he'd had a sleepless night like me. Jahan took a bottle of water from the small fridge and drank from it. I wanted him to leave before his phone rang, and before he started fidgeting around, talking about his own father and all that had happened to him.

I went to the door and signaled, "Jahan, go home." He looked at me kindly and caressed my hair. The knot on my scarf came loose and it slipped to the floor. He picked it up and put it around my shoulders, "I'll go check on things at the office." He gestured to Kāk-Niāz to give him his briefcase, but as he took it, it opened and a few colorful, wrapped boxes fell to the floor.

Before he left he said, "See you later." I smiled and nodded my head.

I looked at my father and his ventilator, pumping oxygen. He was having difficulty breathing. I walked to the window. On the other side of the street I saw Shirin stepping out of the car. She handed Jahan the keys and walked around and sat in the passenger seat. The car took off.

The sky wasn't visible anymore, and nightfall was slowly covering the street.

XXIII

I told Sara, "Good news! A publisher has agreed to publish my book!" Sara yawned again, "How nice! Good job! How'd you find the publisher?" I said, "There are tons of publishers around here. They're not difficult to find." I didn't tell her that Shirin had told me about this publisher when we hung out. I didn't even ask why she was yawning so much! It was already noon their time. I was worried about her loneliness, worried that she smoked when she was out with her friends. One time when she returned home, her red leather jacket smelled of something other than cigarettes. It was the smell of weed! "Sara!..." She raised her voice and said, "What do you expect me to do? Stay home, depressed like you? When people hang out here they smoke weed, but I don't, because it makes me sick." She picked up her purse, went into her room and slammed the door.

The smoke had everyone coughing. Flames circled the classroom's wooden chairs and tables. I ran from one class to another, calling Sara's name. Where was she? I leaned against a wall. I didn't know what was at the end of that long hallway. Where was Sara? Where was I? I heard a police whistle, and cut through the dense smoke. Someone yelled, "Move! Get out of here!" A man wearing a mask took my arm, and dragged me away. Everyone was running. I heard a police officer shouting, "Get out of the building! He is still around!" He wasn't caught yet, he was still roaming in the building, shooting indiscriminately. He was a student. He had smoked weed too. Flames came out of the windows. I was taken to a street behind the university and wasn't sure, where I was, or where I should go.

There was a traffic jam and the cars kept honking their horns. I screamed, "Sara!" but it didn't come out right. My voice was stuck in my throat. I had lost my voice, just like I had lost you and Sara. Just like I had lost myself...

Someone hugged me from behind and kissed my hair and neck, "Easy darling! What's wrong? You're having a bad dream." I took a deep breath and lost myself in the warmth of his skin, and the smell of his breath. I wanted to tell him about my nightmare. I wanted to tell him that I missed Sara, that I missed you... He pressed his warm lips against my ear and didn't give me a chance to speak, "Hush! Try to forget it."

XXIV

With an unbelievable act of compassion, Jahan postponed the party to forty days after my father's passing, as was customary. But in the meantime he went to every party he was invited to, and I was glad he didn't insist on taking me along.

Hiva and mother tried their best to be here, but they weren't able to arrive in time to see my father for the last time. They were on the flight over when he died, but took part in the extensive funeral services that followed. Hiva couldn't stay longer than two weeks and she intended on taking mother back with her when she left. Kāk-Niāz wept, "What will I do ma'am?" Mother tried consoling him, "We'll find a way to take you with us. Don't worry." Mother could no longer live in that house. She said it was full of old memories that she could no longer bear. She gave me a power of attorney to sell the house after she was gone, and I promised to make the arrangements for her to go to Toronto after the forty days of mourning. Hiva went along with all the plans. She, as always, was kind and accommodating.

Jahan said, "Hiva is so much like your mother. She laughs like her, talks like her, and is quiet and calm like her." When I told her this, she chortled. She looked like she wanted to tell me a secret. She looked to make sure no one was around, "Listen! I've been wanting to tell you for some time, Jahan is so similar to Sohrab. Have you noticed?" I said, "You think so?" Hiva was excited, "I noticed a similarity when I first saw him in America, but when I saw him at the airport for the second time; he looked so much more like Sohrab. I thought for a second they might've been related."

Kāk-Niāz appeared, carrying a tray of tea and Baklava. Hiva took a cup. She noticed me shunning this talk.

I was upset with Jahan, and wasn't sure how much longer I could live with him.

Mother walked from room to room, like a wandering ghost dressed in black, running her fingers over the picture frames. Hiva called her, "Mom, your tea is getting cold." She came and sat next to me, holding father's prayer beads. "I wish I had died and never heard the news..." I looked at her. I had nothing to say. My heart felt like bursting with sorrow.

I tried to console her, although I knew it would be to no avail. Then, to change the subject, I asked in a philosophical vein, "Have you ever thought about fate? Do events just happen or are they predestined?" Mother rolled her eyes as if to imply, "What's all this nonsense about!" Hiva and Kāk-Niāz looked at each other thoughtfully. The door-bell rang and Jahan arrived. It was late and I had to go home. Eventually our visitors departed one by one, which left me with an intense feeling of loneliness. I felt terribly downcast for a few days and couldn't bear not having father around.

I had to sell the house as soon as I could and bid farewell

to Kāk-Niāz. Mother insisted, "After you sell the house, make sure Kak-Niaz gets a share too. He has been loyal to us. I want him to have a nice apartment of his own." Kāk-Niāz preferred to buy something in his hometown, Paveh. He had a silky voice and father sometimes sang along with him. There was a unique quiver to his voice that made me nostalgic.

Kāk-Niāz sometimes spoke Kurdish with us. Hiva understood a little but couldn't speak it.

Babak had taught her to speak French. I met him a few times, but couldn't quiet connect with him. Perhaps, it was because they called him Mark and I detested that name. One time when they were on the phone, I heard Hiva call him Mark. After she hung up I said, "Please don't ever call your husband Mark when I'm around. It reminds me of Mark Barton!" Hiva was kind and understanding, "Of course! You're right." I felt bad and hated myself. How could I be so selfish? To change the subject I pointed to father's closet and said, "Should we give his suits to Kāk-Niāz?" Hiva looked sad, "Whatever you say." I said, "Of course he'll have to hem the pants and sleeves several inches!" We feigned an uneasy laugh.

XXV

You and father meshed as soon as you two met. You said, "Dr. Marzban looks so Kurdish, tall with dark eyes." Father laughed and patted you on the back, "Kāk-Zorav my name is Diaku." When mother explained that the Kurds pronounce Sohrab as Zorav, you giggled. You liked your Kurdish name and kept repeating it.

I said, "And this is my beautiful mother. She is either a French or an English Kurd!" You looked at her admiringly, "I didn't know there were any blond, blue-eyed Kurds. And so beautiful too!" Mother blushed and pointed to me, "Take a look at your own wife!" You squeezed me tight, "You're right. My wife is a darker version of you." Hiva cut in, "A black pearl!"

What a wonderful night we had, and the ones that followed when I had both you and them near me. I felt safe and my problems seemed petty and childish. After you fell asleep, Hiva, mother and I, hung out and talked all night. They tried on the gifts we brought them and I tried on the Kurdish dresses they had made for me.

Now, when I look back in hindsight, I can feel a trace of fear or anxiety, which I couldn't pinpoint then. Even Hiva noticed my nuanced mood swings and the occasional anxiety I felt. Every time I stared blankly into the distance, she asked, "Where've you gone again?!"

Hiva was excited about moving to Canada. I joked, "You prefer your friend Roya to your sister?" She smiled, "No, but..." Father signaled me not to take it seriously. He turned to Hiva, "You can go whenever you can get a scholarship like Hannar! Otherwise, there are universities here too." But mother who couldn't bear being separated from another child said, "She's got a long way to go, still..." Hiva knew mother was sad about my leaving Iran, and tried to console her, "I'll come back as soon as I finish school." Mother sighed, "Hannar said the same thing." I protested, "The first few years I had to improve my English and as soon as I got into the university..." You cut in, "Your mother is upset, because you married me and ended up staying there..." Mother was embarrassed, "Oh no! I swear that's not true!"

We all laughed. You placed your right hand on your heart, "I promise I'll send her to visit you every year." And you didn't break your promise...until the last time when Sara and I came together, and Mark Barton entered our lives.

Years later, after Hiva married Babak, a Canadian citizen and left Iran permanently, I asked her, "Do you remember that night? If people knew what fate had in store for them they wouldn't fight and make so much fuss about little things all the time..."

XXVI

A few months after we returned from Iran I found a good job and you also signed a contract for two construction projects. Sara was on her way into our world, and we were about to buy the house on the hill. One day you said, "It's done!" I couldn't believe it. You put the keys in my hand, "All that's left is for you to sign." You took a deep breath, "Let's celebrate. Let's go enjoy a fancy lunch."

The restaurant was crowded and we had to wait long to be seated. I said, "I'm not too hungry." But you pointed at my belly, "That one is!" Two people paid their bills and left, then, the waitress called our name. I was so happy, I couldn't eat. I wanted to go see our new house. I was excited and scared, all at once. How were we going to pay the mortgage, month after month? How were we going to fill the big living room, and the other rooms with furniture? We needed a lawnmower too... You pushed all my worries aside, "I'll take care of it. Don't worry. It just needs hard work and intelligence." I wasn't quite sure what you meant by hard work and intelligence. You smiled, "You will soon enough."

Our master bathroom was amazing. It had a separate bath and shower and a huge mirror. I ran my fingers over the small square green and blue tiles, "It reminds me of Iranian architecture, blue and green..." The windows opened to the back yard with a pea shaped swimming pool and betrayed a wide view of neighboring houses with triangular shingled roofs, sparkling in the sun. During summer, heavy torrential rain fell on those roofs and cooled the hot and humid air.

You stood next to me on the balcony and opened your arms like a bird about to fly, "Just take a look! It's a festival of colors! Such a panorama..." As you roared with laughter you picked me up and twirled me around. I pleaded, "Easy! Be careful!"

There was nothing for us to sit on in the living room, so we sat on the stairway. You were in a hurry to pick a name for the baby. You rested your head on my belly, "Are you a boy or a girl?" I didn't want to find out before I delivered, so we bought both blue and pink clothes, and enjoyed picking out a name.

XXVII

I couldn't postpone it any longer and had to arrange the party before going away with Kāk-Niāz. Jahan didn't plan on joining us and wasn't too fond of my going away either, "You've already given him the money. Why can't he go on his own? He's not a child." But I had to go. I wanted to see the city where I was born, to breathe its heavenly air and relive my childhood experiences.

Jahan called me and we went into the bedroom. He lowered his voice so Kāk-Niāz couldn't hear, although with him humming in the kitchen, he couldn't hear us anyway, "Please don't ask for his help at the party. I have hired a Bangladeshi team of servers." I nodded in assent and went to the door. He called me again, "Are you upset?" I said no, but I was lying. Kāk-Niāz's help in the kitchen couldn't diminish the party in any way, and I wasn't going to ask him to serve the guests in the living room, anyway. But Jahan's inconsideration broke my heart. Especially when my family was gone, and Kāk-Niāz was the only one reminding me of my family. Jahan couldn't understand why we were so keen of Kāk-Niāz and his loyal type, the type he considered the lower class! I never understood his definition of, "our class". I had asked, "Don't you think people's worth is measured by their kindness and understanding?" And he had shaken his head and pressed his lips as if to say, "What nonsense!"

This morning when I told him we were going on bus, he lowered his coffee mug and said, "What?!"

He wasn't interested in being close to common people, and couldn't understand the joy of travelling on bus, moving leisurely through the picturesque landscape, devouring valleys, foliage, wheat fields, and rolling hills covered in tulips and narcissus in early March. I wanted to sit in the roadside tea shops along the way, eat eggs, fried in whipped butter with flat unleavened bread and sip tea from narrow glass teacups.

And talk with the old tea shop owner as he smoked his gallian, water pipe and ask, "How much longer to Assad-Abad pass?" And ask again, "Did you know Dr. Marzban?" and count the lines etched on his forehead as he fell into deep thought and nod my head in assent. And if he didn't know my father, I wouldn't lose hope, I'd ask again and again at other tea shops closer to Sanandaj. "Hello, would you mind telling me if you knew Dr. Marzban?" And someone would finally answer, "Yes. Didn't he represent Kurdistan in the Parliament?" And Kāk-Niāz would excitedly say, "Yes, that's the one!" And the tea shop owner would beam, "Of course I knew him! Who doesn't! He was a fine man. Where did he go? Is he still alive? Did he move abroad? ..."

Kāk-Niāz had peeled and braised the eggplants to such golden perfection that I hesitated mashing them in the dried whey sauce. My only task now was to prepare a few appetizers, as well as khoresht e khalal badam, almond lamb stew, a Kurdish delicacy that Jahan wanted me to make. He had ordered the rest of the food and desserts. As he was preparing the menu I protested, "Just remember this is not to my taste. It isn't how I'd host a party." And he found a way to taunt me again, "I know! You're used to an American menu. You'd order a veggie or a peperoni pizza and have everyone sit around the table, eating pizza by slice and drinking coke or beer by the can!"

Before Kāk-Niāz left for the night, we made plans for Saturday, twenty days away. We planned a trip that would take me away from the commotion surrounding me to faraway, yet familiar places, to Sanandaj and the Uramanat villages with their wild beauty of mountainous landscapes, forever covered in green.

"Miss Hannar, when we reach Paveh you'll feel alive again. We'll head to Shahou Mountain one day, sit on the grass and look at the Sirwan River." When I closed my eyes that night I felt like I was sitting on the foothills of Shahou, listening, as Sirwan flowed by, below us.

Scanty populated, Paveh is known, as the town of "a thousand Masulehs1". It is also famous for its pomegranates. Jahan couldn't believe the city had no intersections or traffic lights. I said, "Come along so you can see for youself." Kāk-Niāz said excitedly, "All its streets are terraced."

I missed the city where I was born and spent my childhood. I missed the time when I thought Sanandaj was as big as the whole world and Iqbal Square was the largest square in the world. I especially missed Farah Street and house number 7, with its green metal portal. I used to stand tiptoed in my new red shoes to reach the door knocker to rap, so Kāk-Niāz, water hose in hand, would open the door to the world's greenest garden.

Mom used to tie a red ribbon around her blond curly hair. And as Hiva saw me she would drop her pacifier and jump into my arms.

I told the doctor, "I despise nostalgia. It makes me homesick. I don't want to think about it, talk about it, or write about it. I don't even like flipping through family picture albums." But sometimes I see the past so vividly that it's hard to ignore...I can hear the water running in a brook. I am holding a wicker -basket picking basil, turnips, and green peppers with Roshana, our maid. But as always, I am

---

1. A village in the north of Iran, built into the mountainside. Masulah has a unique architecture where each roof serves as a courtyard for the house above.

distracted by the coins hanging from Roshana's scarf jingling each time she bends down, or the large flowers on her pleated dress with more color than all my color pencils. Roshana swiftly picks the herbs with her henna dyed hands, singing along to Khaleghi's voice, oozing out of the cassette player. When her baskets are full, she picks both up with one hand, lifts me with the other and carries me to the wooden bed on the terrace.

She puts me down next to Hiva, who is fast asleep on her blanket. Mother has stretched out her legs on the carpet and is carefully putting on nail polish. I look at her and then turn to look at Roshana sitting on the edge of the pool, slicing a melon. I bring my lips close to mother's ear and whisper, "Are you prettier than Roshana?" She ruptures with laughter. Hiva wakes up, and tears fill her eyes. With fresh red fingernails, mother unbuttons her blue satin shirt and I lift Hiva and press her against mother's milk-laden breasts.

After dinner that night, Kāk-Niāz asked to see my father, "Excuse me sir, I want to ask you something." He asked for a week off so he could take Roshana to Paveh. Father asked the reason for their sudden trip, but Kāk-Niāz wouldn't tell him. Mother said, "She is a new bride, maybe she misses her family."

Three days later Kāk-Niāz came back alone. He brought along a sack full of walnuts and another full of Tarkhineh1. Mother asked, "Where's your wife?" but he didn't answer her. To evade her, he started singing and dancing like Kurds do. He stretched his hand toward me, and I took it. This was a

---

1. Mashed wheat cooked with milk that is then made into balls and dried for use in winter.

dance I had learned as a child. Dancing is an integral part of Kurdish life. Once the sound of doholl is heard, men and women start to line up, bend from side to side, and jump up and down.

Late that night, as I was lying on my stomach, drawing, I heard father whispering to Kāk-Niāz, "Why did you do such a thing?" Kāk-Niāz spoke faintly, "She asked for a divorce. She wanted to have children and I couldn't..." I couldn't hear the rest, but when he left, I heard mother chuckle, "Poor girl! She put up with it for six months!" Father returned with a smile, "So that's what it was all about! Interesting!"

XXVIII

I saw you at a classmate's wedding for the first time. Her name was Leila and she was your cousin. I was wearing a semi-traditional Kurdish dress, made of black and red velvet. Leila introduced us and left, "Sohrab, meet my friend Hannar."

I felt a sharp electric shock when I first took your hand and then, I was taken by the sparks in your eyes. You spoke with a Native American accent and if Leila hadn't mentioned your name, I would've never believed you were Iranian. You had on a black tuxedo with a black bow tie and a heavily starched white shirt. You asked politely, "I didn't catch your name, Henna or Hannah?" I replied, "Neither. My name is Hannar." You repeated it twice and asked again, "Where is it

---

1. A large two-sided drum, covered in cow or buffalo hide.

from?" I shrugged my shoulders, "Take a guess."

You were silent a few moments. The music was deafening so you came closer, "France? Italy? Argentina? Or ... I have no idea!" I cracked up, "You're way off. I am Iranian, Kurdish. Hannar means pomegranate in Kurdish." You shook your head and replied in Farsi with a smirk, "Interesting! Beautiful..." "Are you mocking my name?" You laughed raucously and raised your glass, "No! I just wanted to say I really like pomegranates!" The music was louder now and many were dancing. You put your glass down and took my hand gently, "May I?" and pulled me onto the dance floor.

Once the music stopped, I could hear you better, "That was beautiful Hannar. Have you taken lessons?" I smiled bashfully, "No, but thanks! I've liked dancing since I was a small kid."

At the dinner table, you introduced me to your friend Siavash. The music wasn't too loud any longer and we could talk easily. You pointed to your friend, "We were classmates at the university. We both studied political science. When I graduated, I wasn't sure what to do, because I wasn't too interested in the subject. But Siavash continued on. I turned to structural engineering instead..." We began to talk about geopolitics, populism, socio-economics, etc. Siavash was a cheerful man with a sense of humor and he suggested we change the subject. He said, "This discussion doesn't go well with a wedding. It'll give us heartburn! Let's change the subject." You cut him, "But you started it!" I was relieved by Siavash's suggestion, because we had been speaking English throughout and I couldn't understand all you said.

After dinner and cake it was time for the bride to throw her bouquet. But first the groom had to remove the bride's garter and toss it toward the eligible bachelors to tag the next groom. When Leila, in turn, tossed her bouquet, it whirled in the air and was caught in my skirt. Everyone clapped ecstatically and the music roared on. After I said goodbye to Leila, I came up to you with the bouquet in my hands. You demanded, "Now that you caught the bouquet, may I give you my card so you can invite me to your wedding?" I took the card but didn't call you, until you finally asked Leila for my number and called me yourself.

XXIX

I tell Sara that I really miss her. I tell her we have a large party tonight and have even invited a live band. Sara is curious, "What kind of a band? Kurdish or Iranian?"

I know what she means but I can't help correcting her, "Don't ask Kurdish or Iranian. The Kurds are Iranian too. It's a Mexican band with two mariachis. We met them at the Mexican Ambassador's residence, Mr. Pedro."

I take a look around. Everything is ready. The dishes and some of the food have already been laid out. Two of the guests have sent huge baskets of flowers in advance; I fill a few vases with fresh water, just in case more flowers arrive.

Tonight, I plan to primp myself. It feels like a competition. I want to attract the attention of the guests, take their minds off the entertainment and Nazanin and draw it to myself. But how? I wish I could play a musical instrument or sing. I have a decent voice, but only good for singing when I am alone. I have never had the nerve to sing in front of a crowd. Maybe after Farideh sings her corny, melancholic song and after Dr. Reza's droning declamation, I'll recite a poem or two. Maybe something from Robert Frost, or Walt Whitman, or one of the poems I have translated, the ones we used to read together. I don't think Jahan has ever read any poems, and the guests won't understand any of it anyway and will probably make fun of me.

XXX

You looked handsome in your white blazer, but why were you blanched? As I put on my jacket and boots, you kept pacing around our small room that seemed even smaller, packed with our suitcases. I pointed to the wrapped souvenirs on the bed, "Don't forget them." You looked at me, "So much stuff?" I glanced back, "I got a few things for your mother too." Your hands were frozen and you sounded hoarse. You said, "It's difficult to meet her! I could never imagine it!" I asked, "Are you afraid?" You sneered, "Of my mom? Mother's aren't scary." I handed you your raincoat, "Put this on too. Hurry, it's getting late." It was raining. Kāk-Niāz brought us an umbrella, but I said we didn't need one. He tried to console me, "Rain is good omen. It brings luck."

The door opened even before we rang the bell. A tiny middle-aged woman with short silver hair, wearing a black dress, stood in front of us. You stood behind me and I almost had to drag you inside, "Hello!" Your mother stood there in silence, looking you over quizzically. She might've said something, but I couldn't hear anything. She bent toward you and kissed your hands fervently, tears running down her face. You pulled her hands and hugged her. She kept sobbing, "I can't bear to kiss your face."

Her loud sobs brought tears to my eyes too. You looked at her sweetly and wiped her tears with your white handkerchief. I interjected, "Sohrab, your mother is beautiful!" Another woman stood to her side. She leaned forward, "Zari, you promised not to upset them the minute they walked in." Then she turned toward us, "Nice to meet you. Please come in. Sohrab Dearie, I'm your aunt, Zari's sister." It was as if Zari just noticed me, "Please excuse me! I was expecting your entire family Hannar!"

She sat next to us, but her tears didn't stop. Your aunt brought her a glass of sugared water. Zari's hands shook and your aunt kept flipping her prayer beads, reciting something inaudibly. Your mother didn't take her eyes off of you, "It's a miracle ... a holy miracle..."

You didn't touch your food. I said, "All this food, just for the two of us?" I wondered if she was trying to make up for the years she had abandoned her six-month-old child.

I was worried about you turning pale, but you didn't lose your kind smile for a moment. Your mother and aunt were sitting across from us, offering one dish after another. You rose, apologized, and asked where the bathroom was. I rose too. "Are you okay? You don't look well!" You pointed to your head, "I've got a terrible headache." I heard you throwing up in the bathroom. Your mom kept wringing her hands, "Oh my God! He's not well!"

Your aunt nodded sadly, "It's because of all the stress. It's no easy thing Zari!" I heard the faucet turning on and off, and I knocked. You opened the door; your forehead was covered in sweat. You looked at us, "I am sorry. I've got a splitting headache." Your mother suggested that you rest in the room she had prepared for us. You looked desperate, and followed her like a good boy. I had never seen you like that before. I followed you, "Should I call father?" You said, "Not yet. Please go eat your dinner."

Zari brought a bowl of cold water and a towel to place on your forehead. "Close your beautiful eyes and try to rest a little honey..." Your aunt motioned me to go out with her, "Let's go finish our dinner."

Before the door was shut I heard you ask your mother, "Where were you all this time?" I leaned against the wall and closed my eyes. I wanted to cry, but your aunt took my arm and pulled me to the dinner table, "We should let mother and son get acquainted." She put the rosary beads around her neck, "Let's go burn some incense. He is so tall and handsome!" I took her hand, "No, the smoke isn't good for his headache."

Soon, the sound of your sobbing merged with the thunder and heavy rain, battering the windowpanes. Your aunt and I sat at the dinner table, covered with cold dishes, and look at each other in heavy silence...

XXXI

Clad in starched white shirts and black ties, Bangladeshi waiters roam around, holding cocktails and appetizers on round silver trays with the right hands, while keeping their left hands behind their backs. Beluga caviar, fresh caught from the waters of Caspian, is generously spread on petit buttered toasts with a squeeze of lime; tonight they're more popular than the pates au saumons, pate de foie gras, charcoterie, or tabbouleh. Jahan's birthday has passed by a few days, and I have ordered a large tutti fruitti cake. It's supposed to be a surprise. He probably thinks I've forgotten about it, just like last year. He doesn't know this date evokes sad memories for me, and I have intentionally postponed it by a few days. I wear a new dress I bought last time we were on a trip together. I fell in love with its orange hue, the minute I saw it. It is a unique pale orange with a strap on the right shoulder, leaving the left shoulder exposed. I have wrapped Jahan's birthday gift and plan to give it to him before the guests arrive. It's a silk Versace tie matching the color of my dress.

He is stunned when he sees me and looks me all over like he's never seen me before. Then with pursing lips, he whistles. You used to whistle the exact same way! How is this possible? He comes forward and takes the wrapped box from my hands, "You are too beautiful tonight. I'm getting jealous!" And that is exactly what I want; I want him miserably jealous!

The guests begin to arrive. Once again, Nazanin is the last to arrive. I don't know why she likes being late. Maybe she wants to turn heads with her arrival. She is wearing a long white dress. No. It's not a dress; it's a pair of loose silk pants and a beaded cropped top, revealing a generous part of her shoulders and the recess of her lower back. Jahan kisses her on the cheeks and takes the bouquet of red roses she has brought. I hear her whisper, "Happy birthday!"

Did I hear it correctly or am I imagining things? She walks

forward, "Hello! Nice to see you again." The scent of her perfume is awfully familiar. No, not just familiar, it is exactly the same as mine, Chanel No 5! Why do I feel that Jahan has bought it for her? But when did he see her? Where?...

Mrs. Farzad arrives, offers me her hand and looks me up and down. I can't remember her first name. "You look so beautiful darling! We missed you at our party." Now I remember! Her name is Farzaneh. "Thanks so much Farzaneh." I go to the bedroom and wipe the perfume off from behind my ears, and between my propped breasts. Where is my other perfume? The one you chose for me. You said it was called Poem. I liked the name first then, grew to like the scent. I spray Poem all over myself to erase the perfume Jahan had given me.

The living room is crowded and pulsated with good vibes. The guests are actively mingling in groups, small and large, and alternating; talking and laughing animatedly. The Mexican singer can't be heard over the commotion.

I walk toward Mr. Williford and his Spanish associate, Juan, who flew in from Mallorca last night just to attend our party. Mr. Williford bends down admiringly and kisses my hand. He speaks with a thick British accent. Juan speaks Spanish and a few words in English, but with his heavy accent, they don't sound much different from Spanish.

I wanted to learn Spanish when I lived in America. I tell them this and Williford nods thoughtfully, "We sometimes leave things we really want to do for later, but there is no 'later'. Time flies by..." Juan says something and waits for Mr. Williford to translate, "You are still young. Young and beautiful! You still have plenty of time left." I sigh unconsciously and Juan continues, "I invite you to come to

Mallorca for a few months and you will learn to speak Spanish better than you speak English." Jahan comes and stands beside me. He strokes my hair, "Are you having fun?" He brings his lips to my ear and whispers, "Where've you been? They're ready to serve dinner." I announce loudly, "Dinner is served!"

Sasha, the head Mariachi, continues to play the guitar, singing nostalgic songs while the guests are busy eating. His romantic performance feels out of sync with the guests' stuffed mouths. We have around fifteen foreign guests. Dr. Hemmat asks everyone in English to raise their glasses in honor of Jahan and me. Williford raises his glass, "Salute Hannar! The most beautiful hostess in the world!" Nazanin is sitting in a corner, chatting with Mrs. Sadri. What are they saying that keeps them from hearing Williford's praising words? Sasha begins to sing a Cuban song (Guantanamera) that I like while Farzaneh lauds the balsamic vinaigrette dressing. I try to listen to Sasha above the crowd, while Jahan serves Nazanin some Khoresht e khalal badam, almond lamb stew, on her saffron rice. He is probably telling her I made this stew, because they turn and look at me at once. I ignore them and turn to Ms. Stevens.

Dinner finally comes to and end and we rise from the dining table.

Ms. Stevens points to the piano and asks if I play. I wish I did, I wish I had continued playing.

Father bought me this piano, and I used to play quite well. During the last lesson, my teacher, Madam Thomas, turned to mother who always sat with us in the living room, applauding me during class, and said, "See how much she's improved?" Mother's eyes filled with tears, "What's the use?

She is leaving everything behind and is going away!" Madam Thomas wagged her finger at me, "Listen girl! You shouldn't quit playing the piano! Ever! Do you understand?" Although, I didn't know much about American, I tried to reassure them, "I've heard there are pianos in the dormitories. I will take my sheet music with me!"

I turn to Ms. Stevens, who is still waiting for an answer, "Once upon a time I did, but life in America changed everything. I was, either, studying, working, or raising a child..." She asks, "How long did you live there?" One of the waiters approaches us, "Excuse me Ma'am, shall I lay out the dessert table?" I tell Ms. Stevens, "Sixteen years" and blankly walk toward the dessert table.

The guests applaud enthusiastically for Nazanin to perform. In this midst, Jahan, Dr. F., and Farzaneh seem more excited than the rest. As everyone turns silent, and the sound of Nazanin's setar and melancholic voice fills the air, I trace your spellbound gaze in the dim light until I reach your familiar eyes, the same eyes that have drawn me here, eyes that blink with Jahan's eyes, eyes that on nights like this are fixed on another woman; that almost kills me. I feel a fire burning in my heart, a pressure in my head, and a tremor down my spine.

I didn't forget about Jahan's birthday cake that I barely managed to fit in the refrigerator, but I don't bring it out anymore. There are enough hot and cold desserts laid out on the table, and Nazanin already wished him a happy birthday with her red roses, what more does he want? When Jahan leaves for work in the morning, the cleaning staff can have the cake.

Time crawls by slowly, and I'm stuck at my own party with these people; and the melancholy sound of Setar brings out Nazanin's sexy voice that makes your heart beat faster in Jahan's chest. When? When will it end? When will this hellish night end?

I can't remember the name of the taller Bangladeshi server, "What was your name?" He is young and polite. He speaks in such a low voice that... "Aha! I remember. Shabous!" Shabous bends over and fills my glass, over and over again. I can no longer stand on my feet. Finally! It's over! Everyone applauds, but me.

The Mexican band takes over. They begin with an Argentinian song that I love, a song that pulls me up from my seat and draws me toward you and Jahan. Now it's my turn to captivate you with the teasing movements of my body, hands, and legs. With one swift move, I pull the orange scarf from around my neck and throw it around Jahan's. I pull him around like a slave while the guests applaud. He wraps his arms around my waist, and I forget all eyes upon me...until with orange color lips, Jahan leads me back to my chair...

The morning sun has lit up the entire room; I feel happy and content. I look at the clock and feel ashamed. The bed sheets are wrinkled, and Jahan has already left. My beautiful orange dress is crumpled in a corner. For a moment I can't remember where Jahan has gone. Our party was on Thursday night and today is Friday. I think he mentioned something about a trip. He was going away for a few days with Mr. Williford, Juan and a couple of other people. After drinking half a cup of coffee I go into the living room. The cleaning staff has been busy since early morning and everything is clean and spruce. The cleaner, Ms. Mehri, is the doorman's sister. She usually comes with her two daughters and a niece and cleans the place up in a jiffy.

I leave their pay next to her purse, "I've left some food aside from last night for your lunch, there's also an untouched cake in the fridge; take it with you when you leave." She smiles genuinely, "I hope we didn't disturb you with our noise when we got here early in the morning. Mr. Jahan asked us not to wake you up." Once they leave, I feel famished and remember that I forgot to eat last night.

I haven't heard from Jahan by four in the afternoon and his phone is turned off, so I call his office. When Shirin quitted the office, and after I sold my parents' house, Kāk-Niāz began working there, serving tea; running errands. He spends the nights there too. "Hello Ms. Hannar!" I say, "Jahan told me where he was going, but I can't remember now, do you know where he might be?" He replies, "They went to Khorasan, to Nishapur, Birjand, and some other places with the foreigners and Ms. Seyfi." What's he talking about? "You mean Nazanin Seyfi?" His voice sounds amplified, "Yes, that's her. But don't tell him I told you! They went to visit a factory and also Mr. Jahan's friend who makes those musical instruments, what're they called? Tar, or setar, or sitar? I don't know!" I am no longer listening to what he says, and I hang up the phone without remembering if I said goodbye.

The phone keeps ringing all night, and I hear Jahan's voice on the answering machine, "Please pick up darling. Hannar?"

I have the same short, disjointed dreams about Mark Barton again. I dream about the dark veins bloated with blood, throbbing in his temples. I dream of his hands that keep getting larger and larger and his index finger as it moves toward the trigger. I dream of the blood splashing on his white shirt, and of the six hundred, no not six hundred...six hundred thousand dollars that I have borrowed from someone; and the flames coming out of his eyes!

Atlanta is hot and humid, like a sauna. What was the name of that sauna place? Was it called, "Beauty Center"? I said my friend had told me that saunas in Germany were mixed; men and women sweated together. You sneered, "But we aren't that civilized in America yet! Especially in the south!" You dropped me off, "See you in a couple of hours."

I can't find a taxi at the airport, and don't know what to do. Maybe the taxicabs are there but I just can't see them. The sun is blinding my eyes. I take the MARTA train to town, but halfway there it breaks down and the passengers have to get off. The six hundred thousand dollars are in a floral cloth bag, the same cloth we used to sew around eggs a few days ahead of the Persian New Year, before dipping them in boiled water to dye the eggs. I press the bag against my chest and run. I try to stop the cars, but they are passing fast like the wind and don't stop for me. How far is it to Buckhead? How can I reach you? I start running once again, my legs slip from under me and the bills scatter all around, I scream and wake up.

What a terrible nightmare! It felt like dying. I wonder what we'd do if we were doomed to have nightmares after we died, especially nightmares casting Mark Barton as the main character!

XXXII

You were a small child when you left Nishapur, but you had

a distinct memory of the brittle saffron toffee called, sohan, a local specialty there. The last time Sara and I travelled to Iran I called you from Nishapur, "You were born in such an amazing city! The city of poetry, love, wine, and turquoise ..." I asked what you wanted as a souvenir and you quickly replied, "Sohan!"

Your mother insisted on buying plane tickets to Nishapur for Sara and me, she also made hotel reservations for three days. She wanted to show us the house, where you were born in. In Nishapur, she bought us turquoise and necklaces, and a ring and prayer beads for you. I joked, "Just imagine Sohrab with his prayer beads in a business meeting with his American colleagues!" The three of us laughed about it for quite some time. Your mother's eyes were black even in the sun and had nothing in common with yours. Every time we mentioned you, she cried admonishing herself for the years she had lost you, I sympathized with her and tried to cheer her up, "When I go back, we'll buy a nice three-bedroom house to have plenty of room for you. Sohrab will send you an invitation letter, so you can obtain a visa and stay with us for the winter."

You said cheerfully, "We've been lucky, I have invested some money in the stock market and it has almost doubled. It'll probably grow more by the time you return. The market is on a bull run!" You kept sending us pictures of houses you saw and called us every night, "Why do these July days go by so slowly?" I felt the same way. I desperately counted the days till seeing you, but I couldn't make it earlier, because I didn't want to break everyone's heart here, my parents, Hiva, Kāk-Niāz, and of course your mother, who loved Sara so much.

It is the twenty-ninth of July; the flight from Nishapur to Tehran has a two-hour delay; the airport is hot and humid; the air-conditioners barely work; I am anxious, and tired of Sara nagging. Days like this when I don't talk to you like I want to, are frustrating. The telephone connection in the hotel was bad, and the three or four times I called you, all I heard was, "The connection's bad, call back from Tehran please."

I feel better once we board the plane; the air-conditioners are in full blast; Sara fastens her seat belt and quickly falls asleep. I feel like I am one step closer to you. By the time we arrive in Tehran it is early evening.

Father is sitting on his prayer rug; motionless; mother and Kāk-Niāz are in the kitchen. The entire house smells of steamed saffron rice and fried eggplants. Sara runs and hugs father from behind. I put my bags down, "I'll go take a shower." Hiva comes to the bathroom door with a clean towel, looking unwell. "Are you sick Hiva?" She hands me the towel, "No, I'm fine." She leaves and shuts the door. As the water soothes me, I think maybe she's been arguing with father as usual. She is generally meek, but sometimes she can't hold herself from saying things that she shouldn't. I turn the water on all the way and take a nice long shower. I enjoy taking showers in Iran. When I was in America, I was anxious when I showered, especially during winter. Our water heater was electric and electricity was expensive. You and I worked hard those days to save money and fantasized about a trip to Iran as if it was a dream...

Sara started daycare early on. I dropped her off in the mornings, picked her up early evenings and hurried home to prepare dinner. And you constantly worked long hours. You signed a contract with another construction company, but like most other folks we knew, we worried about losing our jobs. Sometimes you begged, "Let's go out to dinner tonight." And while I wanted to, I dissuaded you, because our income left no room for extravagance. You persisted though, "Pick up honey! It's me!" and I hurried to pick up the phone and make up an excuse, "I've made a delicious dinner, I know you'll love it, see you home soon."

The 1987 market crash in America ruined many lives, especially the lives of those who heavily traded in the stock market. They went bust, lost their livelihoods, defaulted on their mortgages and lost their homes too. For those unfortunate ones in Atlanta, the magical city once home to Margret Mitchell's "Gone with the Wind," all was gone with the wind again…just like our home on the hill…

When I step out of the shower I smell the scrumptious food mother has prepared and feel hungry. But first I need to call and hear your voice. Mother calls me and points to the sofa, "Sit down here Hannar honey, drink this first and relax…" She hands me a cup of borage tea, I take the tea and sit down. Father comes and sits next to me, holding his prayer beads, "So… how was your trip?" Kāk-Niāz brings father a cup of tea also. Hiva takes Sara out of the room as mother takes a few tissues out of the box.

XXXIII

I disconnect the phone so I won't have to answer Jahan's calls. In his last message I heard the sound of daf and dotar1.

---

1. Traditional Iranian musical instruments

They were probably at a pleasant local spot after a day of sightseeing, and they're probably enjoying a lamb kabob dinner.

I nervously pace from one end of the living room to the other. I have to leave before Jahan is back. Before he looks at me with those eyes and shuts my mouth with those lips, before he can tame me like the poor lamb he sometimes buys to slaughter, and before he plays the lover's role in this unfair game.

I call Kāk-Niāz and tell him we'll travel to Kurdistan sooner than we planned. He sounds happy, "Whatever you say! When?" I reply, "Early tomorrow morning."

Once again, I start pacing the living room, talking to myself, asking and answering questions. I am alone...alone... alone... How can I finally realize I am alone? Jahan is nothing more than a bubble, a dream, a misunderstanding, he is a stranger, he is not you, not you ... Maybe he stole your voice one night, one dark night when the stars were asleep, he stole your gaze, your lips, your arms, your body, and your secrets ... ... like he stole you from Sara and me ... Mark ... that damned monster Mark ... ouch!

My hand doctor ... be careful! Don't squeeze it! No! ... I told you, I didn't fall. I hit it against the table. Well, I got mad and slammed it hard...

We couldn't leave yesterday because of my hand. Kāk-Niāz came over early this morning and stared at my bandaged hand. I point to the suitcases, "Don't worry. It's nothing important. It's just a bruise." He asks if I've had anything to eat and I tell him we'll have breakfast along the way.

As the taxi heads to the bus terminal, I take a deep breath. I am glad we managed to leave the house before Jahan returned. And the pain in my hand is not that bad.

At the first tea shop along the way Kāk-Niāz puts a breakfast tray in front of me and starts eating his fried eggs, rolled in lavash bread with insatiable appetite. I meanwhile wonder what color eyes Mark Barton's had? I have seen many pictures of him, but I can't remember the color of his eyes!

Kāk-Niāz keeps talking and I keep nodding my head without listening. He says, "Some people change their color." I believe some people change the color of their eyes. Hiva wouldn't believe me, "You're imagining things!" Sara said, "So what? What difference does it make..."

XXXIV

We had a four or five hour layover at Amsterdam's Schiphol airport. I rushed to the newsstand, bought Sara a chocolate milk bar, and a copy of the Times with "SHOOTING IN BUCKHEAD" written in large font on the front page. My heart sank. It was about the shooting in Atlanta's Buckhead. Oh my God! And here was your picture next to the other innocent victims, people who woke up one morning and left their homes in fear and shame with thoughts of their families and the monies they lost on their minds.

The news of the stock market crash and the loss of fortunes had driven many mad. Those who hurried to the Brokerage House at Piedmont Center, in Buckhead, to see if the news, that had once killed them before they were shot in cold blood was true or not, were speechless. "Yes it's true! Take a look at the damned computer screens." The Times recounts the shooting vividly. Mark Barton's name and his picture are all over as are the names of those murdered. But thank God! You are not listed among the dead. They hadn't lied to me after all; mother, father, Hiva, or Kāk-Niāz. They said you were shot and in the hospital. Father's face was white with pain and the circles under his eyes were darker than usual, "Hurry... go to your husband." He comforted me, "Don't worry about anything, I'll help you leave tomorrow evening, I'll arrange your ticket!"

And I left the next day, while finding a ticket on such short notice wasn't easy.

XXXV

We are riding through the Assad-Abad pass, turning and turning with the ever turning road, Kāk-Niāz, the mountains, the road, the bus, and I; and I think to myself what would it feel like to fall down into the bottom of these deep, mysterious ravines? Will it only last an instant? Or will it be full of pain, sorrow, and anxiety?

Like the days I plunged down into the abyss when Jahan lied to me; and Shirin lied to me, and I saw them through the hospital window as my father was taking his last breaths; and that horrible mourning...

It's like it was just yesterday.

Some statements sound like clichés but they are true.

Things like, "I'll forgive but won't forget!" It was during a time when all my family had left Iran, and I was busy selling my parents' house. It was Friday evening. I had plans to meet the buyers at the house and Jahan said he'd stop by the office. After I finished my meeting I didn't feel like going back home. So I went to Jahan's office and parked across from his car. I pressed the buzzer again and again, but no one answered. I pressed it again, and again, and again...

I pressed it one more time and kept my finger on the buzzer. I saw light through the window. I got worried and didn't know what to do. As I was about to press the buzzer again the door opened.

Shirin appeared at the door. She had a cigarette lit between her fingers. I didn't know she smoked. She had told me that she occasionally smoked when she had a drink. She kept her head down and didn't look in my eyes. I asked, "Is Jahan in?" She moved aside without a word.

I hurried in. Jahan's office reeked of Shirin's perfume, and the smell of tobacco and coffee. He wasn't at his desk. He was lying on the sofa with his shirt unbuttoned. Two coffee cups were on the table in front of him. I just looked at him. I couldn't find a trace of you behind the thick smoke coming out of his mouth. It was like you had died inside him.

I slammed the door, got into my car, and sped away. Villa's Pastry Shop was almost empty; two elderly Armenians were cozily sitting in a corner talking to each other. I ordered coffee and sat down; I looked at the street for a while, at the people passing on the sidewalks, at the cars, motorcycles, and the old Church on the other side of the street. I tasted the coffee, it was bitter, I got up and left, I can't remember if I bought any pastry or not. When I reached home it was still early evening. I felt like seventy restless birds were fluttering in my chest. What should I do? Should I go visit Sara? Leaving won't change anything. I didn't feel an ounce of joy inside me to share with my daughter. I picked up my pills and a glass of water, they calm me down.

I heard the door open and shut. Jahan walked into the kitchen as confident as ever and sat in front of me. My pills and a glass of water were on the table between us. I looked at him. He cleared his throat, "I didn't know you were that sick! You are truly delusional! You should see a psychiatrist!" I raised my voice, "She has to leave the office! You have to fire her!" He raised his voice, "That's impossible! You can't interfere in my work!" I raised my voice higher, "Shame on you! You lying bastard!"

His shouting matched mine, "You have no right to come to my office unannounced!"

By this time I was yelling, "You have to fire her!" "That's impossible!" And right before his eyes, I emptied all the pills in my mouth and swallowed them. He just looked at me, picked up his briefcase calmly, went to the TV room and shut the door. I heard the newscaster's voice, followed by a singer whose name I couldn't remember. I saw through the bedroom window, the city turn dark. The trees looked like phantom spirits, twisting and turning in the wind. And then everything went black...

I look at my watch. Jahan should be on his way back to Tehran by now. Or maybe he has extended his trip for a couple of days, but I don't think so, Kāk-Niāz doesn't either. He wouldn't leave the office to the new secretary. There are other employees, but as Kāk-Niāz says, none of them can compare to Shirin who was amazing at her job.

I think of plunging to the bottom of the valleys...I have to leave him. I have to get rid of my thoughts, and then, I have to get rid of him...

We go through a few more turns and reach a narrow road with wide-open fields dotted with an occasional tree on either side.

When I opened my heavy eyes I couldn't see anything, except for white tiled walls, and a hose that went through my mouth, all the way to my stomach, filling my intestines with water. I fell asleep again and woke up moaning and hallucinating. In the leaden room I saw a man sitting in the corner with his face in his hands, his shoulders shook as he quietly wept. I thought the woman sleeping in the hospital bed next to me with an IV in her arm might be Marie-Thérèse, and the man in the corner might be Picasso. But then, I remembered that Marie-Thérèse didn't take pills, she hanged herself, and Picasso never wept for any woman, not for Marie-Thérèse, Françoise Gilot, or any of his other women.

Kāk-Niāz wakes up in the front seat, turns around and looks at me. I murmur, "People forgive but they don't forget." He doesn't understand, "What did you say?" I just shake my head. After a while, I hear him, audibly, cracking sunflower seeds. He is singing to himself, he has black wavy hair, and I wonder if he dyed it, because it shows no sign of aging. But the wrinkles on his forehead and the corner of his eyes betray his age, he has looked like this for as long as I can remember. My mother used to say his face was always smooth and never needs shaving. He offers me some sunflower seeds, "Why don't you sleep Ms. Hannar? You'll be sick if you don't." I take a few sunflower seeds and point to my watch. He says, "We're almost there. Take a nap and we'll be there soon."

It's an early evening like all other early evenings. A fly keeps, tenaciously, buzzing around my face. One of the passengers is peeling cucumbers and sharing it with the person sitting next to her. A baby is crying in the seat behind me, her mother tries to comfort her with cooing sounds; she gets up, sits down, and moves the baby around to get her stop crying. The other passenger offers her a peeled cucumber. A few of the passengers comment, "The baby is tired, it's been a long trip." A husband and wife are sitting near the bus driver; they haven't said a word to each other the entire time. Kāk-Niāz whispers, "I know them, they are married, I heard them quarreling, they're not talking to each other." He's probably right. They've been looking out the windows on opposite sides the entire way.

Jahan isn't into the silent treatment; he handles the situation with flowers and gifts; with the innocent look in his eyes he can justify anything, even shifting the blame on me. But he, taking Nazanin along on this recent trip without telling me about it, can't be forgiven. I won't answer his calls anymore; I will end it all and go live my own life; I have made a decision and it calms me down.

Kāk-Niāz gently shakes my shoulder, "Wake up." The bus pulls off the road and alights at a small café. The driver says, "We'll make an half-hour stop." We get off the bus; the air is clean and cool. A flock of sheep and goat come down the hills with two young boys and a sheepdog, goading.

I miss Sara, I miss you too. We had wanted to come here together, to breathe the delicious air under these beautiful skies. To visit the orchards, fields, farms, and villages up close; to stroll through the towns and shops at the local bazaars. Mother said we'd all go together, so father could show you the land and tell you about its history.

Kāk-Niāz brings two cups of tea and a few lumpy sugar cubes. I'm sitting on a wooden bench outside the café and he is sitting on the grass, drinking his steaming tea. Then he looks at the hills in the distance and begins to sing; he has a soothing, melancholic voice. I feel sad, but it's not just because of his voice.

The bus driver calls the passengers. Kāk-Niāz continues to sing and some people gather around him; one of the passengers begins to sing with him. The driver calls again, and Kāk-Niāz swiftly jumps in the bus and says Hello to me. "We're almost there, we'll change buses in Kermanshah and from there it's only a short distance."

Kāk-Niāz is in good spirits; he chats with the other passengers and laughs. He turns to me again, "I can smell Āvāz's lamb stew from here!"

Āvāz is his sister; we met long ago when she was a child. I think she is around my age, "When did you manage to tell Āvāz we were coming? We left so suddenly!" He chuckles. I look at my mobile phone, which is still turned off. I wonder if Kāk-Niāz has broken his word and turned on his phone. When we were having lunch today he stepped out of the café and looked like he was going to call someone or answer his phone. Jahan will call him without a doubt; maybe he's done so already. I don't want to know. I'm glad Kāk-Niāz hasn't told me anything.

I close my eyes and think about my decision again. I need to breathe the air that Sara breathes. If being close to the old memories ails me again, I'll move to another state and find a job, but where should I go? I have to keep it a secret for now.

The bus comes to an abrupt halt. Kāk-Niāz gets up, "Let's

go Ms. Hannar, we've arrived in Kermanshah!"

XXXVI

The plane lands hard and comes to a slow halt down the runway. I am incredibly anxious. We've been travelling for almost twenty-four hours, but this was the first time that I didn't want to arrive. I feared reaching our destination. I was afraid of seeing your wounds. Were you still in pain? Were you bleeding? Where had you been shot?

The passengers rise from their seats and begin removing their bags and parcels from the overhead bins. Sara is happy and excited. She pulls on my shirt to tell me something. I bend down. "Is dad picking us up?" I reply, "No, Leila is picking us up." I pull Sara and the carryon bag. I try to walk fast, but my knees shake and my legs are heavy. Each time we returned from a long trip, I'd run through the airport to see you as soon as I could.

I miss you so much, I won't feel right until you take my hands in your kind hands and kiss my fingers like you always do.

XXXVII

I have just fallen asleep when there's a knock on the door,

"Excuse me!" I can't remember where I am. I feel dazed and don't know the time. I jump up in bed and look for a light switch, "Yes?" "Sorry to wake you, your husband is on the phone. He's called several times. There is a problem with the guest phone and you haven't answered your mobile phone. Can you please come downstairs?"

Oh my God! He's going to drive everyone crazy all night long! I should turn on my mobile phone. Kāk-Niāz can't keep his mouth shut! My phone rings just as I turn it on. I pick up and hear his voice, "So what now?!" I remain silent. "Hello?" He sounds admonishing. I don't know what to say, "I was tired. I was asleep, what do you want?" He lowers his voice and sounds affable, "I was worried. Why're you acting so childish? We were going to visit a factory with Williford and his friend, and Nazanin came along to meet the folks from Birjand and buy a couple of musical instruments. Hello?" I am still silent. "I bought a nice one for Sara. I thought she might like to learn to play some day."

It's all nonsense. He must've had a drink and is lightheaded. "Are you listening?" I don't feel like answering him. "I miss you Hannar. Why did you take the bus? Couldn't Kāk-Niāz go on his own? You've all spoiled him..." I drink some water to keep my voice from breaking, "Listen, Kāk-Niāz can go anywhere he likes. You don't seem to understand, the reason I left is to get away from that house, from you and all your secret games! Do you understand?"

He raises his voice, "Hang on a second! Listen to me. I may forget to tell you about some things you don't need to know, but I am not into keeping secrets! Why? Because there is a reason for everything I do. People lie because of fear, and darling, I'm not afraid of anyone or anything..." After a short pause, he bursts out laughing, and I have to move the phone away from my ear. I only say, "Good night!" and hang up. I turn off my phone. I keep tossing and turning in bed. The streets are empty and the moon looks like it is hanging off a walnut tree.

As soon as I fall asleep I start dreaming of Mark Barton. Each time I wake up with a start, I can feel a cold sore growing on my lip. In my dreams I see you with your sunglasses and white shirt, parking the car and stepping out. I am standing there right in front of that damned stock trading center. I try to come to you but my knees won't bend. My screams are silent too. I lift my arms and wave over and over again, but you don't see me. You walk right past me into building number 301. Two minutes later, Mark Barton walks in like a whirlwind, a hurricane, a tornado...and everything is, "Gone with the Wind,"...

I don't hear the sound of the bullets. I can't hear them, because the images in my dream are silent. The day it happened I was in Mashhad, buying you sohan.

I wonder if people like Mark Barton go insane because they've lost six hundred thousand dollars, or if it is pathological. Instead of, buying a pair of shoes, or a sandwich, they buy a handgun, a rifle, or a grenade. If he hadn't been surrounded by the police at the BP gas-station and hadn't shot himself, I would've asked him, why didn't he kill himself before shooting all those innocent people and his wife and kids?

I wake up with the phone ringing. It seems the guest phones have been fixed. The sun is pouring through the blinds, lighting the room in stripes. Is it Jahan or Kāk-Niāz calling? I don't feel like talking to either of them and don't know what time it is. I am supposed to meet Kāk-Niāz around two o'clock.

XXXVIII

The air is crisp and clean and a slight breeze rustles the leaves. The scent of fruit and flowers fill the air, just perfect to spend hours walking through the wide and narrow terraced alleys.

But our destination is not far. And we reach it shortly. Āvāz and one other woman are waiting at the door. I don't know who the other woman is, but they both greet me, kissing me on the cheeks. Kāk-Niāz says, "It's Roshana, don't you remember her?" I can't believe my eyes; she looks so weathered and thin. What happened to her beauty? "What are you doing here?" She hugs me again, tighter. She bends to kiss my hands. Kāk-Niāz says, "She is like my own sister." Roshana blushes, "Ms. Hannar, I am so glad to see you." Her face still has faint traces of beauty, but she has changed much. When I was a child I found everything about her interesting, her clothes, her laugh, the way she hung the laundry, and the way she cut melons. After she left I missed the sound of her jingling bracelets, the clinking of her scarf coins, and her hennaed hands among the parsley, turnips, and peppers.

Āvāz has spread a feast-like lunch on the floor. She invites me to sit at the top, on a soft white cushion, next to a fan, surrounded by small colorful pillows. One of her daughters has recently married, and she talks about the wedding, as she keeps filling my glass with herbed buttermilk. Roshana tells me she has two sons and a daughter. Her daughter is pregnant again. I ask, "How is your husband?" Her eyes fill with tears, but she smiles and says, "He's fine." I look at Āvāz. "Her husband turned out a foul character. When he first married our Roshana, he had a shop in the bazaar. But then, he joined the freedom party and they shut down his shop. He began to work as a street peddler. He sold turnips and fava beans in winter and pomegranates in the summer. And when he was drunk he beat the children. Once he turned them black and blue, he'd regret it and would beat himself. With three kids, he had a hard time making ends meet..."

Roshana weeps as Āvāz recounts her fate. I look at her, "So how is he now? Is he better?" Roshana swallows, "One day I woke up and he was gone, he ran away and left us."

The lamb biryani is served in a large, round copper tray and placed in the middle of the spread. The steaming saffron rice over lamb roasted in leaf lard, smells delicious.

We take a stroll in the afternoon. We cross a bridge and sit by the river and later, reach the walnut and pomegranate orchards. Roshana left after lunch, but Āvāz accompanies us on the walk. The three of us speak in Kurdish, reminiscing about the past, and I begin to remember Kurdish words I'd forgotten. By the time they drop me off at the hotel it is already dark.

I keep thinking about Roshana and can't fall asleep. Her life is so similar to that of Fred and Käte Bogner in Heinrich Boll's novel, "And Never Said a Word", except that they lived in Koln after World War Two, and she lived in Kurdistan after the Iran-Iraq war. In that story, the man affected by the horrors of war and the ensuing poverty is also angry and frustrated and takes out his anger on his children by constantly beating them.

I stay awake in bed for a couple of hours, thinking about poverty and its affect on people. I think about the authors who have written about this subject like Hugo, Darvishian, and Zola, until I slowly fall asleep.

A few days later I say farewell to Kāk-Niāz and Āvāz and continue on to Sanandaj to spend a few days in that city and its surroundings. That night and for the following two weeks, my nightmares about Mark Barton keep returning. I feel weak and tired. I spend the days walking through streets and bazaars like a wandering spirit, taking the same paths I used to take as a child. Kāk-Niāz calls every day, but most of the time I have my phone turned off. Then one day I'm fed up with all of it, the polite servers and nosy guests at the hotel, the shopkeepers, the steps that take me from room 212 to the dining room, the streets, here and there and back again. I want to go back as soon as I can and anyway I can: plane, car, or wagon. I will even walk if I have to.

I feel like flying over the hills and mountains and the winding roads to get rid of Mark Barton's leeching presence behind the thick burgundy curtain in room 212. I want to go faster than the car he is driving, to get there before he pulls the trigger, and tackle him hard. I want to stand in front of him and scream, "Don't shoot!! You ruthless bastard!"

And then, you and the others who are on the floor in terror look up at me in amazement. The police arrive, sirens blaring, and take away Mark Barton, his gun dropped to the floor, crying like a baby. You and I are breathing hard from excitement. We run toward each other, entangle in each other's arms, and go back home to live our life together and begin everything anew.

Early the next morning, the cab driver puts my suitcase in the trunk and drives me to the airport. I call Kāk-Niāz to say goodbye.

XXXIX

Leila, your cousin, was the first person I saw at the airport, followed by our close friends Yassi and Behrouz. Your other friend was there too. The one you called Sia. Why were there so many people? Just for us two? Sara and I...? I blurted out, "Is everything okay ...?" Sia took my bag and said, "Why shouldn't it be?

I was still confused when Leila whispered, "I'll take Sara; you go with them." She picked up Sara in her arms and left. Yassi and Behrouz opened the door for me to step in the car.

Sia handed me a chilled bottle of water, "Drink! You look hot and sweaty!" I opened the bottle, "Which hospital is he staying at?" Yassi uttered, "St. Joseph's." I asked Behrouz, who was behind the wheel, to go to St. Joseph's.

My hair clip was dangling; Yassi fixed it for me, "I think we should go home first so you can take a shower and refresh yourself before you see him." I tapped Behrouz on the shoulder, "No, go to the hospital first! Please take me to St. Joseph's!" Behrouz nodded silently while Yassi kept telling me to drink. I didn't feel like talking to any of them, "Why did all of you come to the airport?" Sia quipped dryly, "We came to get the souvenirs you've brought us!" I thought to myself this is not the time to joke.

I asked, "Where was he shot? Is he still unconscious?" Yassi pointed to the bottled water and said, "Drink more. You'll see when we get there." I raised my voice, "Just give me a straight answer! Is he still unconscious?"

Behrouz stopped at a gas station and turned off the car. He opened the back door and came and sat next to me. Sia lit a cigarette. Yassi and Behrouz hugged me from both sides and the sound of my screams and their weeping brought my world to a halt.

Those moments of being out of time, out of place and empty, were weightless. One felt like falling asleep, but a sleep without dreams. It was like the month of May in Kurdistan, when I slept in a cradle hanging from an almond tree, as my grandmother sang Kurdish lullabies and the first name she taught me was,

Sohrab:

A panacea, and you have arrived after Sohrab's death

Oh stone-hearted, you might have come sooner, why so late

My father loved you like a son from the moment he hugged you, and said, "Kāk-Zwar welcome!" And Kāk-Niāz kept burning wild incense, whirling the smoke around your head. He confided later, "He caught the evil eye!" and I retorted, "So your incense burning rituals were good for nothing?" He dropped his head, "It shames me!"

XXXX

Mother has promised to come and see me, but obtaining a visa is not easy, especially for those who have already applied for a Green Card. She calls every day, even if she has nothing new to say.

I still live in the same apartment we rented years ago. The rent keeps rising every year but I work fulltime now, which has the added advantage of helping me fall asleep from exhaustion in front of the TV, every night.

Sara opens the door before I have a chance to take out my keys. I wonder why she is here? Maybe she has come to take some clothes or shoes. She says, "Hurry up, call Grandma, she has some good news for you." I make the call. "It's finally done sweetheart! Your father sold his office today!"

For the past few years I have been hearing that my father is not able to see many patients anymore and the office is closed most of the time. Mother is very excited, "Our lawyer says our Green Cards will be issued soon. We are supposed to go to Turkey next week, and then, ten or twelve days later, God willing we will..."

Mother's news was a blessing in those bleak, dreary days. But my father was not coming. He had made up his mind and wouldn't budge, no matter how hard I insisted.

"Why don't you return to your homeland? I won't come to a country where guns are displayed in stores like clothes and shoes. Where any crazy drug addict can buy one any time he pleases! No darling, don't argue with me. I have seen that place once, and that was enough!"

Father's wound didn't heal after what happened to you, and it never would. Some wounds cut so deep that even if they heal, they will always leave a scar. Father is still talking, but I am thinking about you, "They keep talking about human rights! What sort of human rights allow just any one to have a gun, claiming it's the law?!" I don't know what to say. I keep my mouth shut and remain silent when he is in such pain. He finally comes to the point, "Your mother is coming in ten days. She'll have a travel partner and won't be alone. I want you to meet Dr. Akhavan's son."

I had never met Dr. Akhavan, but I knew he was one of the shareholders, and also the hospital director, where my father practiced, "Is Dr. Akhavan still alive?"

He sighs, "No, he passed away. It's been almost a year." Father says goodbye and mother takes the phone again, "He is travelling to New York for on business, but he is coming to Atlanta first to visit a friend. His name is..."

I look at Sara, "Can you believe it? Mother is finally coming!" Sara screams with joy, "Awesome news! I'll see her again after eight years!" I add, "If she sees you by yourself she won't recognize you." Sara jumps up and down happily and comes to stand beside me, "Let's see who's taller! See! I'm as tall as you now!" She does this every few months.

I make an appointment with my therapist a few days before mother's arrival. He's the only one I can talk to comfortably, "I should probably be happy that mother is coming. And I am. But part of me is not. I am a little sad and worried. My mother reminds me of a remote part of my life that has passed. A part that... it's difficult to say. I mean I love it, but it also disturbs me. It's a part of my life that sometimes I can't feel anymore. It died a long time ago. I always miss it, just like I miss Sohrab... I think seeing mother will remind me of Sohrab's absence even more." I wipe off a tear, and the doctor gently nods his head, "What else? What else is bothering you now?"

I had to say it. I had to overcome my fear, "I am afraid that before my mother arrives, another Mark Barton who has lost his job, or has argued with his wife, or has lost his money, or is drunk, or something like that, comes out of the blue and shoots Sara or me in the head. And then, when poor mother finally gets here full of hope, she'll find a bunch of people in the airport, who force her to drink cold water and take deep breaths!"

The doctor adjusts his glasses, "Nothing can stop an accident dear! Why do you worry about things before they actually happen? Why think of things that are out of our control?" This reminds me of a poem by Forough Farrokhzad, which I translate for the doctor, "It always happens before you think about it".

It is raining when I walk out of the clinic. The trees, cars, buildings, the earth and sky, all smell of life. I drive through the streets with a sense of lightness as Albinoni's Adagio plays on the stereo.

Sara has been living in the university dormitory for a few months now and has a Russian roommate named Natasha. On the day she was moving out, I didn't let her take all her stuff. I thought if she left some things behind, she'd have to come back home more often and I'd get to see her more. It was a bleak, cloudy Sunday. With much effort, I mustered a smile as we said goodbye. But after she was gone...

I spend all day shopping and cooking. I prepare Sara's room for mother, and as the hours slip by, the excitement of seeing her grows. Hiva calls later that night, "I was sure you wouldn't go to sleep early tonight. Is everything ready?" Luckily I have two days off, "It's almost done. The stew needs another thirty minutes on the stove. Mother picked a good day to come."

She asks, "What are you making? Green herb stew or eggplant stew?" Hiva knows I'm an expert cooking these two dishes, because they are Sara's favorites, "I can't make green herb stew. The smell will linger on for days. I have already cooked the lamb shank and fried the eggplants and tomatoes on the stove. I will cook the rice tomorrow. I have also made beef lasagna for Dr. Akhavan's son. I'll finish it in the oven tomorrow."

She says, "Yummy! I'm getting hungry. Is Dr. Akhavan's son coming to your apartment too?" I turn off the stove, "We'll bring him over from the airport for dinner. He's promised father that he'll accompany mother all the way home!" Hiva laughs, "Good for you! I wish I were there too. Babak bought my ticket today. He found a good deal from Toronto to Atlanta for just $300. I'll see you next week."

XXXXI

Jahan is standing right in front of me when I get off the plane. I think to myself, "Another one of his strange antics", and also, "I told that stupid Kāk-Niāz to keep his mouth shut!"

He takes my bag and we walk toward the exit in silence. His driver is here, "Hello Mrs. Akhavan." I muse, "I am Mrs. Habibi, not Mrs. Akhavan!" I feel dizzy and lightheaded. The smell of gasoline and smog sicken me to my stomach. But when he sits beside me in the car, I can't help, but feel safe and secure. My temples throb, with a splitting headache. Jahan notices that I'm not feeling well. He takes my hand, "See what you've done to yourself! You have a fever!" He leans my head against his shoulder and I don't resist it. I don't know if I'm falling asleep or fainting...

XXXXII

Sara and I, arrive at the airport thirty minutes before the plane lands. We both keep looking at our watches, waiting with excitement. But time passes slowly when you are waiting. Maybe this has something to do with some mysterious levers that control time and space. I want to share the idea with Sara, but I don't, because she will look at me with a sarcastic smile and say, "You're philosophizing again!"

The passengers begin to appear, adding to our anticipation. I'm never tired of looking at passengers in the airport. I tell Sara, "Each passenger is a character in his own book." Sara raises her arm and waves, "There she is! Grandma! Grandma!"

Before I spot mother, my eyes are drawn toward a familiar face. The man stepping side by side with my mother looks awfully familiar. He looks like a man carrying you inside of him, with his smile, eyes, and the frown on his forehead. He is even the exact height as you. How is this possible?! I grab Sara's hand. "Sara! Sara! Do you see that guy?" She looks at me questioning, "The one with Grandma? What about him?" Sara always disappoints me. She never sees the things I see. Of course she was very young back then and maybe she doesn't remember you well.

Mother reaches us, "Sweetheart! You've gotten so thin!" I hug and kiss her. Her skin and hair smell of my homeland. I take a deep breath as Sara hugs us both, "Your mother is here! So why are you crying?" I laugh and turn to face mother's travelling companion. She introduces us. I would've never believed that one day my mother would be introducing us. You are standing to her side, waiting, and don't take your eyes off me. Everything seems ridiculously surreal. This world...

this game... and the people who have no choice but to play the game. "This is Mr. Jahangir Akhavan. He is Dr. Akhavan's son. He has been very kind to me." Mother takes Jahangir Akhavan's arm, "Let's go!"

We put mother in the passenger seat, and Sara and Mr. Akhavan sit in the back. I keep looking at him in the rear view mirror and say to myself, "I wish your name were Sohrab! Sohrab is better! Sohrab Habibi."

Mr. Akhavan says, "I gave your number to my friend so he can call you for your address and come pick me up. His name is Faramarz Atabaki." I stare at him in the rear view mirror. Sara loudly repeats what he says, "He says his friend's name is Faramarz Atabaki." I start the car, "Of course. That's fine." I start driving home. Sara talks to mother about me, about herself and her roommate, and mother talks about father, Kāk-Niāz, the neighbors, and the terrible food they were served on the plane.

Dinner has turned out great and everyone likes it. Mr. Akhavan tells us about his travel plans. He talks about his contract with an export company and about the differences between German and British universities. He confuses me. I try not to pay too much attention to him. Mother keeps yawning and her eyes begin to droop. Sara and I, help carry her things to her room. We both hug her before putting her to bed. She is upset that the souvenirs she has brought are still in her suitcase. Sara comforts her, "Don't worry. I'll come back tomorrow night grandma." I correct her, "Don't call her grandma! She is not that old yet!" The three of us laugh.

After we leave the room, Sara whispers, "She looks so old and thin..." I say, "Did you see the veins on her hands?!" Mr. Akhavan hears us, "Don't judge her by how she looks tonight. She is probably tired." Sara picks up her bag, "I'm late. I have to go." She leaves, and I bring some tea for Mr. Akhavan and myself. I feel the warmth of his gaze on my skin. I sit to the side to avoid his direct gaze and then I bring up a general topic for discussion, to keep him from asking personal questions, "So how are things over there? How is life in Tehran?" He talks about things that aren't that important to me. I look at his hands, his watch, and notice the absence of a wedding band on his finger.

I wonder what happened to your wedding band. I kept it on me for a long time, but then, Sara asked to have it. She wanted to keep it as a reminder of you. Mr. Akhavan talks about hiking in the Darakeh mountains on Thursday mornings when Faramarz Atabaki finally rings the doorbell. I stand up and say, "Your ride is here!" But deep inside, I don't want him to leave so soon. We could've spent some time alone, drinking wine, listening to music and talking. We could've even stayed silent, filling and emptying our glasses and occasionally swirling them in our hands.

When we walked into the apartment, Sara and mother started chatting ceaselessly. I filled his glass and he looked at me, "You look very familiar to me." He said, "It's like I've seen you before!" I wanted to say, "Me too." But I didn't. I felt my face blushing and I turned to the refrigerator to escape his eyes.

He stands up the second he hears the doorbell, picks up his bag and his suitcase, and presses my hand warmly as he says goodbye. But his eyes won't leave mine. We spend a few moments in silence before he shuts the door and leaves.

It's one of those nights when I can't fall asleep despite being terribly spent. I keep twisting and turning in bed. I feel like he came all the way here to make me anxious; to sit there for a couple of hours and pretend to be you. To dress like you, walk like you and smile like you, and to make me forget all about mother. I was baffled by the stark resemblance all night long!

As I'm lying in bed, I see the grey sky through the window and the poplars and pines under streetlights. The scent of rain seeps through the crack in the window and floats over my bed sheets. I hear mother's door open and close, followed by the sound of the toilet flush. She is probably sleepless from jetlag and I should go and ask her if she wants something to eat, some cornflakes or a banana or anything else. But my eyelids are heavy and sleep finally carries me away.

Today is Sunday, and I can spend the whole day with mother. I empty her suitcases and hang her clothes in the closet. I blow-dry her hair, file her fingernails, and through it all we chat and call a few people. My father calls twice and each time we say we wish he were here too, and he says he wishes we were there instead, "Listen Hannar darling! You have to find an apartment or a house to buy right away, so you don't have to be a tenant anymore. Do it while your mother is there. I will send you the money."

Mother hangs out in the kitchen, arranging the things she has brought with her: pistachios, saffron, baklava, manna pastry, small yellow candies, sumac, curd, tarhana, etc. I ask, "Why have you brought so much tea? Look at all the tea I have."

She turns on the electric kettle, "Throw those out. They are no good. This is from Lahijan; it's mixed with Ghazal tea. Just smell the leaves!" Hiva calls. I hand the phone to mother and go to my bedroom.

Without wanting to, I keep waiting for him to call to say he had a good time last night, that dinner was delicious... or something like that... I want to see him once again to make sure I wasn't imagining things last night...

Mother comes in with a cup of tea on a tray, "Where did you go? Come have some tea and baklava with me." I take the tray from her. She suddenly remembers her travel companion, the person who has been occupying my mind since last night. "What time did Jahangir leave last night?" The phone rings. The ID display says 'Faramarz Atabaki'. I answer, "That's him!" I hand the phone to mother and pick up my cup of tea. The tea is hot and a few drops spill on my hand. Why am I running away from him? Am I scared that he'll sound like you on the phone?

Mother comes toward me holding the phone, "Okay son. I am still a little hazy from travelling. Talk to Hannar." I take the phone, "Hi!" I can't believe it! I am shocked. I don't hear what he says and what I say in response. I remain silent, and he thinks we've been disconnected, "Hello?" I mumble, "Yes, I'm listening." I want him to keep talking....in the voice that's so familiar to me. It is your voice. The voice I used to hear in the quiet privacy of summertime, lost in pomegranate orchards...

I'm sweaty when I finally hang up. Mother looks at me with curiosity. "What did he say?" I try to be calm. I shrug my shoulders and walk toward the refrigerator, "Nothing. He wanted to thank me for dinner, last night. He is going to New York tomorrow, but when he comes back he'll call to see us again." Mother chews on the baklava, "He is very wealthy. And such a gentleman. He is into export and import." I try to change the subject, "Tomorrow is Monday. You'll be alone all day. You can look through the photo albums. I leave at eight o'clock and come back home around five or six." She picks up the crumbs from the kitchen table with a tissue, "Don't worry about me. I know how to entertain myself." Then she looks at me, "Tell me, are you done seeing a psychiatrist?" I smile reluctantly, "I don't go as much any more. I have stopped taking pills, but I still see my therapist once a month. It's pretty expensive." Mother grumbles, "Oh my God! Just see what Dr. Marzban's daughter has come to!"

I peel an orange and put the plate in front of her. She acts like a child and won't look at me, "I don't want it!" I laugh out loud and kiss her forehead. "I told you I'm fine. I don't take a single pill anymore. Don't you believe me? You should've seen me those days..." Mother sighs and tears start flowing from her blue eyes, "I sent my lovely daughter here to study and come back home!" I put the box of tissues on her lap, "Mother, please!" But she won't listen; tears keep rolling down her soft, white cheeks, "It was your fate sweetheart! Of all the people, you married an unlucky man who was shot by a bastard, turning my daughter into a widow!" I look at her and caress her blond curly hair. I wish I could cry as easily as she does. I close my eyes and listen to her. The phone rings and Sara's cheerful voice saves me, "How are you guys?! Are you having fun?" After I hang up the phone I turn to mother, "Sara is on her way over. She will be here in a couple of hours. Please don't say anything while she is here." She cuts me off, "Of course not! I'm not crazy! Don't worry."

Father has sent me the money from the sale of his office. He wants me to use the money he earned working and seeing patients all those years, to buy an apartment in Sara's name. He wants me to take a vacation and rest a little. He wants me to accompany mother back to Tehran, so he can see me again. Mother is listening to what I say, "Memories of my last trip still pain me." He admonishes me, "You'll never be able to wipe out that memory until you come here one more time."

I change the subject, "How are the neighbors?" He answers, "Do you mean Zari? She sold her apartment that year and went away. I've heard she's gone back to Mashhad." I feel sad. The poor woman had just found her son! After what happened, I called her a few times, to no avail. Her sister would pick up the phone and say she was not well and couldn't bring herself to talk to me. I ask mother why she didn't think of asking for her new phone number and address. After all Sara is her granddaughter.

Mother, standing in front of me, begins to talk with resolve, "Why would I tell you about her? Why would I want to remind you of that poor soul again?" I plead, "Please let's not talk about it anymore." She rises, and looks me straight in eyes, and says reproachfully, "Stop fooling yourself. How long are you going to run away from the truth? It is over! Try to forget it! Think of yourself, of your youth..."

We lighten up when Sara arrives. Mother laughs to Sara's witty quips. I can't believe she is the same woman, as the one she was an hour ago, the same one who wept and cried and threatened me. After dinner, mother asks Sara when will she be coming back to see her, so she can cook a Kurdish stew for her. And then, she tells us a few jokes in a Kurdish dialect, which brings more laughter to her than us. When Sara is fixing to leave, mother says, "So soon? I was just about to sing you a song. It's okay, I'll do it next time." Sara kisses her, "You are so much fun grandma! I love you!"

After Sara leaves, mother looks at me, "Come Dearie!

Sing something to make us feel better. Why have you changed so much? Do you still play the piano? Madam Thomas asked about you."

Mother and I used to sing well. We used to sing duets, while father drank, and slowly munched on yoghurt and cucumber dip. Kāk-Niāz would sometimes join in with his Daf, turning our small gathering into a musical show with Hiva dancing along.

XXXXIII

Sara arrives as I 'm making dinner. Mother is happy to see her. I murmur, "Thank God you're here, now I get to see Sara more often!" Mother has been here for only a week, but the mood here has changed completely. As I strain the green beans and begin roasting the potatoes, mother takes Sara to her room. I hear Sara's voice, "More souvenirs for me?! What's going on grandma?!" Mother says, "This is not a souvenir. It is my own necklace and I want you to have it." Sara comes out excitedly, "Hannar! Where are you? Take a look at this!" I remember mother's necklace quite well, "Those are rubies. They look beautiful on you." She hurries back into the bedroom, and I hear mother, "There is a much bigger gift for you from your grandfather." The dryer goes on the spin cycle, and I can't hear anything more. I turn off the stove and take the clothes out of the dryer. As I pass by mother's room, I hear Sara's voice through the closed door, "What a good idea. You should take her to Iran with you. She drives me crazy on Sundays, spending the whole day at the cemetery. And she never goes anywhere in the evenings, not to a park, not to visit anyone, or anywhere else. She keeps saying she's not in the mood." Mother consoles her, "I'm sorry. It seems she won't let up until she drives us all crazy."

Hiva arrives the following day and I hand mother over to her and take a break. They rent a car, spend the days shopping and sightseeing and usually arrive home a little before I do. Hiva works in Babak's computer firm, so she doesn't have to worry about taking time off. She is planning to stay here with us for a month. I ask my friend, Lisa to show them a few apartments, to buy. Lisa has a good taste, and after I tell her what I am looking for and what areas I am interested in, she goes to work. On weekends Hiva and my mother take me to see the apartments they have screened. It doesn't take more than a couple of weeks to decide on one. Father calls daily, asking how our search is going, and when we tell him we have found a nice apartment, he is overjoyed, "Have you signed the contract?" I tell him we are going to do it tomorrow. "Thank God! I can stop worrying now and you can stop working so much, just to pay rent."

It is a three-bedroom apartment with a nice view of a park. Mother loves it, "It's newly built, cozy, and sunny! Your current apartment doesn't have any sunlight. How could you live here all these years?" She says, "An apartment without sunlight is worthless. It is depressing."

All goes well quickly and we buy the apartment in Sara Habibi's name. We'll be moving there in three weeks. Sara loves the apartment, but she is hesitant to move back and live with me, no matter how much her grandmother, her aunt, and I insist. "I'll fix a room for myself in the new apartment, for when I visit, but I prefer to stay at the dorm." But mother won't let go, "Tell me why? Don't you love your mother?" Sara is upset, "Of course I love her! But I can't live with my mother at this age!" Mother looks at Hiva and me in surprise. Hiva laughs, "But you just turned nineteen! You're not that old!" Sara looks at her watch, "I'm late; I have to go."

After she leaves, mother keeps staring at Hiva and me, "Don't you dare tell your father; it will sadden him, the poor man..." and then she begins to comment on, "this strange land" and goes into her room, where she shuts the door and begins to weep quietly.

I look at Hiva and whisper, "I'm glad you're here." She takes my hand and presses it. She knows what it's like to live in America and how second generation Americans, born and raised here, won't abide by the old world traditions. They prefer to live independent lives. But this is hard for mother to understand and that's why she is distressed. On days like this, I feel so weary that I can't bring myself to move. But Hiva knocks on mother's door and goes in.

Mother starts again, turning to Hiva, "What a miserable luck! What a miserable world!..." Hiva tries to calm her, "Mommy darling!" But it's as if she can't hear her, "We were fools to send you two away, to the land of Sohrab's murderers..." Hiva tries harder, "Please mom, calm down so we can talk. What would we do if your blood pressure rose again?! You have no health insurance here."

I get up. My legs feel heavy. I pour myself some jasmine tea, and try to hear what Hiva says, "You have to accept it mom. It's not just Sara. Kids who grow up in this culture..."

The tea nauseates me and I pour it down the drain. I go into the bathroom and turn the shower on. There is nothing more soothing than warm water... its warmth...its sound... I try to remember the only Farsi song you knew, "... those black eyes..." I begin to weep and the sound of running water muffles my sobs. I dress and wrap a towel around my head. I feel sorry for my mother. She came here with so much hope. We have to take her out tonight; seeing Christmas lights might cheer her up.

When I step out of my bedroom, mother faces me with her arms, wide opened. She hugs me the same way she used to when I was a little girl. I don't know what happened while I was in the shower, but she kisses and caresses me. I look at Hiva, "What's going on?" Hiva makes mother some apple puree with rose water, "She just feels bad for you!" Mother continues, "Yes, of course I feel bad for you. For you being lonely... for you not having anyone around... how long are you going to sit here and stare at the door, hoping for Sara to come visit for just a few hours? What sort of a life is this anyway?" She takes my hands and pulls me toward her. She lowers her voice as if she's going to reveal a secret, "Do you know what my granddaughter, whom I love dearly, told me yesterday?" I look at her with curiosity. She swallows hard as if the thing that Sara told her has stuck in her throat, "I'm only telling you this, because I want you to face the facts." I wonder why she doesn't get straight to the point, "So what did she say?" She nods thoughtfully, "Wait! Have some patience! She loves the new apartment, but she said she will move there only after you returned to Iran. She said she can't wait until that day! Do you hear me?!"

I look at mother. Her face is contorted with pain and worry. I look at the bags under her eyes, the wrinkles on her neck, and her well-formed lips that keep talking, "You should think of yourself. Leave her to the grace of God and come stay with your family for a while. You can come back to visit her anytime you miss her, or you can send her a ticket to come to Iran."

The phone saves me; I pick up, "Hi! How are you? Are you back? Tonight? No, we don't have any plans..." Mother is smart and knows who it is. She gestures to me to accept the invitation. "With pleasure. Where?" I hang up the phone. Mother and Hiva look at me, expectantly, without blinking. "Hurry up and get ready. Mr. Akhavan invited us out to dinner."

Hiva and I go into my room. Mother calls out from her room, "Come and tell me what to wear!" I reply, "Wear something warm. It's cold tonight."

The waitress is a young, slim brunette. She leads us to a table next to a window with a nice view of city lights. Jahangir Akhavan and Faramarz Atabaki stand up as they see us. Jahangir greets mother and Hiva first and shakes their hands. He then turns to me, and looks at me in silence for a few moments. I hear him whisper, "I can't believe it." He squeezes my hand, takes my coat, and asks after Sara. I begin to feel the same way I did when I first saw him in the airport. I feel like I see you with your loving eyes and your warm smile. As if you stand here, holding the seat for me. I take a deep breath and glance at mother and Hiva who are talking and laughing with Mr. Atabaki; I turn toward the window and look at the Christmas lights. I am absorbed by you, and feel you are absorbed by me too.

Hiva leaves a few weeks later. My mother also prepares to leave, and when Jahangir Akhavan calls once again from Tehran, I ask him the question I've been asking myself since that night. "What did you mean that night at the restaurant when you said you couldn't believe it?" He laughs, "I didn't think you heard me, because I almost said it to myself." I remain silent, waiting for him to continue. "I have seen you before." I am taken aback, "Really? Where?" He goes on, "In a dream at night, on my birthday! You were wearing the same black dress and that same delicate turquoise necklace. It was your face, your hair, those black eyes, and the same loop earrings. What can I say! I dreamt of you exactly like you looked that night! Even the way you were looking at me... hello?" I am shaken, "I'm listening."

"Ever since that dream I was sure that I would someday meet you somewhere. The first time I saw you at the airport, I thought that was it. But you wore jeans and shades and your hair was tied in the back. It was a little different from the image in my dream. But that night at the restaurant, it was exactly the same."

I've no desire to cozy up to him or any other man, but I can't help asking his birth date. He responds, "The 29th of July..." What?! How could this even be possible? He must be playing a trick on me, "What did you say?" He repeats it louder, "The 29th of July in..."

How can this be true? This is the date of the shooting....

I call Hiva. "Can you believe it? Can you really believe it?!" Hiva has been taking meditation classes for some time and is into eastern mysticism. She says with confidence, "Of course I believe it. Herman Hesse says, 'Nothing is accidental.' I hope you don't disappoint mother, go back to Iran with her even if it's for a short time. Will you go? Will you Hannar?" Like someone promising to jump off Mount Everest I return, "I'll try!"

XXXXIV

We arrive home; the driver carries my suitcase to the door. Jahan is holding my arm. He opens the door and says, "Welcome home honey!" I am feverish and giddy. I look around and wonder if we've come to the right place. The living room is bare and nothing looks the same. "Where is the furniture? Where is everything?" Jahan kisses the top of my head, "I gave it all away. Didn't you say you didn't like any of it? Now you can design it any way you like. But you have to rest first and get well." Jahan helps me take a warm bath, puts on my night gown, and tucks me in bed. I feel like a lost child, who has come home after many sleepless nights. I feel safe and secure in my own bed and stay there for an entire week, having feverish dreams. But I no longer have nightmares about Mark Barton. I often wonder to myself, "What happened to Barton? Where did he go?" And I answer mockingly, "Maybe he's away on vacation."

All the while, I get closer to Jahan. He calls in a doctor to see me, and keeps checking on my fever. He makes me soup and fresh juice and brings me red roses and CDs that I like. Our relationship grows deeper.

Since the night I returned home, he has told me time and again, "I can't live without you, Hannar. You don't know what I went through in the twenty days you were gone. Don't ever leave me again!" I look at him with some doubt and smile warmly. I prefer not to say anything about my future plans just yet.

Jahan wants us to redecorate the living room before our next party, which is four months away. Mother will be back by then to move into her new apartment. I buy low, comfortable, colorful sofas for the living room and cover the floor with a few simple rugs. When I hang the last painting on the wall, I finally feel like this is my own home. Our home. You, who are and aren't here. Before Jahan entered my life, you were missing too, and now that he is here, you have confused me with your being and not being...

Jahan returns from a four-day trip to Vienna and when he sees the new decoration, he looks excited, and I can't help but laugh. He loves it all and says it can't get any better, "I love the lighting, and the Ficus tree, and the way you've broken the straight lines with some of the chairs and lamps..." He says the house seems bigger and brighter than before, and I agree.

He mentions the party again and how his friends will be surprised by the changes. The thought of the party and having to see Nazanin again, deprives me of sleep that night and I try to come up with excuses, so he can change his mind about the party.

I finally fall asleep as dawn breaks, thinking about my upcoming trip and my new life faraway from here, under wide-open skies that don't hide any secrets.

A week before the party I visit my mother and invite her too. "No darling. You young folks have a good time. Your aunt is coming over and Kāk-Niāz will be here too. We'll watch TV together." But she promises to come over soon and I'm not sure how I'll be able to say goodbye to her again in the near future.

Mother likes her new apartment and is settled by now. Kāk-Niāz brings me tea and sweets. He sits down on the floor next to my chair and starts humming a Kurdish song that my father liked. Mother translates the first verse into Farsi and her eyes fill with tears, "My homeland's soil is the kohl that adorns my eyes..." I am moved by Kāk-Niāz's kindness and affection. When mother returned to Tehran, he came to see her, his arms filled with souvenirs. He said he'd sleep in the kitchen if he had to, but he couldn't bear being away from us. He said he wanted to stay with us as long as he lived.

I reach home, and Jahan tells me that Sara has called several times. I am worried. I dial her number and ask, "What's wrong honey? Is everything okay?" She sounds affectionate, "Everything is fine. But I miss you so much. I want to know if you'll be coming to see me?" I lower my voice, "I will honey! Soon!"

There are days the sun shines brighter than others. The skies are bluer and the birds sing sweeter. Everything and everyone is in harmony. You receive good news. You are told that your book is in its third print, and they ask you to sign a contract for a new book. And Sara says, "Your room here is ready for you!" And that night you can't fall asleep from all the joy you feel. The wind is blowing outside, bending branches left and right. You look at the clear sky through the window and catch the moon, bright and silver, shining among so many stars. You get out of bed, sit on a sofa in the living room and wonder if these objects will miss you when you are gone.

XXXXV

This time, I plan the menu for the party myself. It is simple and different. Jahan seems more accommodating lately, as if he has decided not to disagree with everything I do. He has set aside his usual conceit and love of display. He seems to have completely changed, and I wonder when and how it all happened, and why so late. Today, I feel like I can even make him change his mind about having the party, but don't. Instead, I promise myself to be kind to all these people, whom I will soon be leaving forever.

Most of the guests arrive around half-past eight. As usual, Nazanin is the last to arrive. Jahan takes a Setar and a guitar from her hands and tells her something that brightens their faces. Nazanin, like the other guests, complements the changes to the house, "I thought I was in the wrong place at first! They tell me you did this all. You are truly talented!" I like to ask who told her, but I don't. She has cut her hair shorter, and seems to have gained some weight.

Jahan pays her no attention all through the evening, not even during dinner. Nazanin talks with the other guests. Then, she walks toward me and sits next to me, "I hear you have other talents too. Did you play the piano before? Why don't you play anymore? If you decide to start again I know someone who..." I cut her off, "My teacher is still around. She is old now, but... I have to finish translating my new book first. It's not a bad idea though. Thanks for the suggestion." I like the idea. Why didn't I think about it before? I turn to look at the piano and can feel Nazanin's eyes on me.

The dinner table is cleared when the doorbell rings. Jahan looks at his watch. Some people ask if we expect anyone else. I tell them I don't think so. Jahan opens the door. Two people carry in a beautiful cake with candles on top and set it on a round side table. I look at Jahan questioningly; he had promised not to say anything! he smiles mischievously and shrugs his shoulders. The guests applaud and drink to our health.

The cake cutting ceremony, followed by Nazanin playing and singing her usual songs, finally come to an end, and the guests prepare to say goodbye. With the sudden sound of a spoon, tapping on the table, all heads turn toward Jahan. I wonder what he is up to now. "I have a surprise for Hannar tonight. I hope she likes it."

My feel my heart, drop. I wonder what sort of a surprise he has in store for me. I'm anxious and Dr. F. almost screams, "Hurry up and tell us what it is! We're dying of curiosity!"

Everyone laughs, but Jahan is awfully calm, "This surprise was a secret between Nazanin and I..."

Everyone laughs again and my heart pounds harder. I can't take it anymore. "About eight months ago, I asked her to take me to her music class. I took every opportunity I had to take lessons and to practice. Hannar was my only inspiration, because I know how much she loves music. She has a very nice voice too. I sometimes listen to her, furtively of course!"

Mr. Sadri stands up, "Let's hear it for Jahan!" The guests applaud. Jahan takes off his jacket, loosens his tie and removes the guitar from its case. He gestures me to dim the lights. I sit at the furthest corner of the room. Jahan sits on a stool across from me. The guests gather around. He is unmindful of their clappings. He tunes his guitar while I strain to wear a smile and try to breathe. Everyone is silent now. Jahan's fingers fly over the strings and he stuns us with a Flamenco piece. I can't believe it, and neither can his friends. Dr. F. is ecstatic, "You play like a pro!" Someone else comments, "Why did you hide your talents from us all this time?" Another person agrees, "How can anyone learn to play like this in only eight months?" Nazanin looks at me with pride and claps. Her new haircut with the, thick bangs over her eyebrows don't suit her much. I smile back. I feel awful for rushing into judgment about her. Jahan seems to be in a different world. He lifts his glass to someone sitting away in the dark and resumes playing.

Most of what he plays sound familiar, but he also sings along with some of the songs and he sings well. I wonder why I had never heard him sing before. And then... what is he doing to me? Is he playing a game on me? I jump up impulsively. No! It's not possible! This song... this song... this is my song... this is your song... with that same rhythm, that same melody, that same voice!

I feel a shock running through my entire body, "Your two black eyes..."

I close my eyes and open them again. It's all real... this room, these people, this song, and I am not dreaming. "... your two loose braids..."

I feel weightless, in the air, suspended. I'm drawn again toward the man sitting across from me, loving him deeply. "... sometimes life is a test..."

Maybe like Juan Preciado, who madly went from village to village in search of Pedro Páramo, I also have been searching for you so madly that I never realized I died too. And maybe tonight, you've come to tell me, this is the other world, the world of the dead, the world filled with people who have died, who don't realize they are dead. I scream inside, "Are we dead or alive?!"

The lights are suddenly turned on, hurting our eyes.

The guests are up, saying goodbye and I take a deep breath.

After the last guest leaves, I turn off the lights, one by one. The starlight is enough to reveal the chaos in the living room. I see your guitar leaning against the silent piano in the living room.

Before going to the bedroom, I walk toward the piano and open the cover. I run my fingers over the keys and whisper, "Listen! Starting tomorrow we're going to work hard together! Before Sara arrives."

Atlanta
Winter 2017

Also By Mehri Publication

Memoir

The Trouble Maker ● Mike Payami

Persian Letters ● Mehrdad Rafiee

Research - History

The Forbidden Tale of LGB in Iran, A Comprehensive Research Study On LGB ● Kameel Ahmady

The Right to Primary Education for Children with Disabilities in Iran ● Parastoo Fatemi

The Forgotten Conquerors (Tales from the castle of the moat) ● George Sfougaras

Kings, Whores And Children: Passing Notes On Ancient Iran And

The World That We Live In ● Touraj Daryaee

Children's Books

Dalí und der geheimnisvolle Spiegel ● Khosro Kiyanrad\ Translated by Sarah Kiyanrad\ Illustrated by Hajar Moradi

Where is My Home? ● Hajar Moradi

I Am My Brother, I Am Not My Brother ● Alireza Mahadavi-Hezaveh\ Translated by Arash Khoshsafa\ Illustrated by Fatemeht Takht-Keshian

My Doll ● Fariba Sedighim

The Padlock ● Ana Luisa Tejeda\ Illustrated by Nazli Tahvili

Who Is the Strongest? ● Feridon Rashidi\ Illustrated by Sahar Haghgoo

Charli in the Forest ● Rasheell Barikzai

Baby Grandma ● Shiva Karimi

Namaki and the Giant ● Ellie I. Beykzadeh

| **Dog and The Long Winter** | by **Shahrnush Parsipur** | Translated by **Shokufeh Kavani** | **£17** | **322 page** |

'From the moment I read the chapters that translator Shokufeh Kavani sent to me, I was impressed by the literary quality. I was struck by the mood and atmosphere of Dog and the Long Winter. It has a haunting quality that lingers on after reading the novel. I found myself drawn in and the novel was totally absorbing.'

——— Sharon Rundle; editor

|**The Legend of the Passageways of the Sandstruck Villa)** | Written by **Donya Harifi, Translated by Arash Khoshsafa** | First edition, 2019 | 146 pages | Price: **£12** |

Every time I cross the threshold of the hall, a seriously strange feeling obsesses me, the sense of getting stuck in a dead end, an eternal dead end. I feel I can never get back.

Persian Letters | **Mehrdad Rafiee** | First edition, 2019 | 554 pages | Price: **£18** |

This memoir is written in the form of letters addressed to Mehrdad Rafiee's sons. Mehrdad tells his life story, with diversions into Persian/Iranian history and politics, drawing parallels between the turmoil in his country and that in his life. In writing his memoirs, Mehrdad was inspired by the books of two very special writers: Orhan Pamuk's Istanbul: Memories and the City, and Azar Nafisi's Things I've Been Silent About. For anyone familiar with modern Iran, Persian Letters will inform and entertain, as it explains much that lies behind the changes and the culture of Iran and its people.